ENTICED BY AN ALIEN WARLORD

Fated Mates of the Ferlaern Warriors 1

AVA ROSS

ENTICED BY AN ALIEN WARLORD

Fated Mates of the Ferlaern Warriors, Book 1

Copyright © 2021 Ava Ross

All rights reserved.

Cover art by Natasha Snow Designs

Editing by JA Wren & Owl Eyes Proofs & Edits

AISN: B0924VCTDN

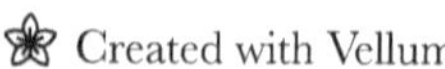 Created with Vellum

Foreword

A note to the reader.

If you found this book outside of Amazon,
it's likely a stolen/pirated copy.
Authors make nothing when books are pirated.
If authors are not paid for their work,
they can't afford to keep writing.

*For my mom who
always believed I could do this.*

*For my family, who puts up
with take-out & dust.*

*Special thanks to
Alex, Deonne, Jenny, Joy,
Kristin, Laura, Meg, & Stephanie
for helping me make my books the
best they can be.*

He has tusks and a tail and insists she's his fated mate. She's enticed but determined not to get involved. Can a burly alien warrior and a single mom find love together among the stars?

Garek: With my clan threatened, I don't have time for romance with a pesky Earth female. Until I meet Piper. She and her youngling son are part of our planet's new settlement. Soon, I find myself helping her plan her home and talking about odd Earthling activities. What is a square dance, and must I do it? She's soft and lush in all the right places, and I could pick her up and carry her around with one arm. And her son… I ache to show him how to tame a mighty winged trundier. Piper may say she doesn't need love, but I'll do whatever it takes to win her heart.

Piper: I brought my eight-year-old son to Ferlaern to start anew—the new wild west, we're calling this planet. The other women want romance but not me.

Then I meet Garek, a seven-foot-tall, gruff warrior who's out to steal my heart. Burned in the past, I'm afraid to trust. Never mind that he makes my son laugh for the first time in forever or that his kisses… Not going there. But when our settlement is attacked by vicious creatures, it'll take both of us to survive the threat.

Enticed by an Alien Warlord is Book 1 in the Fated Mates of the Ferlaern Warriors Series. This stand-alone, full-length romance has on-the-page heat, aliens who look and act alien, a guaranteed happily ever after, no cheating, and no cliffhanger. Look for the series on Amazon.

Books by AVA

MAIL-ORDER BRIDES OF CRAKAIR

Vork

Bryk

Jorg

Kral

Wulf

Lyel

Axil

Gaje

(companion novellas in one book)

BRIDES OF DRIEGON

Malac

Drace

Rashe

Teran

Kruze

(A prequel novella free with

newsletter sign-up)

IN LOVE WITH AN ALIEN ANTHOLOGY

Neere,

a Brides of Driegon short story

ALIEN EMBRACE ANTHOLOGY

Skoar

a Brides of Driegon novella

***

FATED MATES OF THE FERLAERN WARRIORS

Enticed by an Alien Warlord

Tamed by an Alien Warlord

Seduced by an Alien Warlord

Tempted by an Alien Warlord

You can find my books on Amazon.

Before
PIPER

Two years ago, a disease swept across Earth, killing most of the adult men. The women on Earth mourned and tried to find a way to go on, but it sure wasn't easy.

Until a ping reached us. Aliens existed. At first, we worried they'd attack, abduct us, or try to take over our planet. But they came in peace. Treaties were formed, and technology was exchanged. Then the aliens proposed something eye-popping. Since they lacked women and we had so few men, why not arrange matches? Geneticists did their thing, and discovered we were compatible. Those interested in getting to know the aliens were given translators.

A few groups of women traveled as mail-order brides for aliens on a planet called Crakair, and when these matches were successful, more arrangements were made with a race called Driegons living deep below Crakair's surface.

Now another planet has sent us a message.

We are the Ferlaern, a noble race. Hunters, warriors, and riders of mighty, winged trundier. We are fearless and passionate.

Here is our offer: Settle on Ferlaern, and we will court you. Seduce you. Win you. When matches are made, we will provide for you and our young.

So, talk about arrogance. Fearless and passionate, huh?

We posted the message on social media and took a vote to decide what we should do. Some women were intrigued.

Including me.

These are our stories…

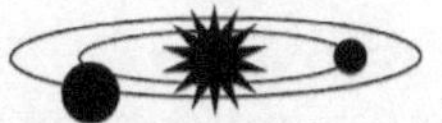

Garek

"Will you mate with one of the females, Garek?" my friend, Durran, asked in a gruff voice. We stood on a ledge jutting from the top of the Woondral Cliffs, overlooking the broad valley where the Earthlings were unpacking and sorting building materials for their new settlement.

Once the other clan leaders arrived, we'd fly down for simple introductions. Tomorrow, we'd start building their square structures made of synthetic materials that might hold back the weather but wouldn't withstand the other dangers in our world. We encouraged them to settle in our mountain village, but the Earth emissaries insisted on this wide, open valley.

I shifted my feet, stirring dusty soil beneath my boots. Caught by the wind, it scattered, making my trundier, Veskar, snort behind me. A reassuring word from me, and his brittle wings dropped back along his sides, his claws clacking on the ledge.

"I don't know if I will mate with one," I finally

said. "It would be a challenge while they live here. I'm not even sure I want to lie with an Earthling. If I did, I want her to live in my domit. They're comfortable, warm, and secure from threat. This plan of theirs is…"

"Odd?" Durran said with a laugh. His lips curved across his tusks, and his tail swept back and forth behind him.

"Why insist on constructing homes here? Such an exposed location."

"They may enjoy being on display. After all, they're female, a rarity here on Ferlaern."

After the horror of our beloved females dying, these few precious beings would attract attention. Many males would overlook their insistence on living by themselves.

"They are vulnerable, though the duskhorde seem to be behaving," I said.

"So far."

I grumbled. Yes, so far. I had a plan for the duskhorde, though. "If they're wise, they'll split up among our clans and settle within our communities. Then we can get to know them and decide if any will fit."

"Are they wise?" he asked.

I didn't have an answer. I've yet to meet any of them. "It will be good to have mates and fledglings around again, but I doubt an Earthling will make my second heart start beating."

"You mean the maelstrom?" His sharp gaze shot my way. "True bonds are forbidden if you become a warlord."

I stood a better chance of becoming a full warlord than of finding a maelstrom mate. A maelstrom demanded time I was unsure I'd be able to give.

"No Ferlaern has achieved a maelstrom for a long time," I said.

They became rare even before our females died. Cycles ago, something changed, and we weren't able to determine what was different. But after that winter, no more maelstrom bonds were formed. We mated, and our females gave birth to fewer fledglings. Many died before they were fully grown.

"Our males are eager to meet them, even if there isn't a chance for a maelstrom bond," Durran said.

This was why we waited here before winging down to the valley for introductions. A representative from each clan would arrive soon, plus my nemesis, Skydar.

"Once I—" I bit off the words, refusing to state my thoughts.

"Once you have become a full warlord."

"Then, and only then, will I consider a mate. I'm as eager as any other male to see my seed take root in a female. Our race will die without younglings."

New blood would revive our clans.

"What are your thoughts?" I asked. "Will you seek a mate if your second heart doesn't beat for one of the females?"

He said nothing for a long while, and I glanced his way, taking in the scars on his otherwise segmented, bronze skin. The lines cutting through his neck, face, and chest—courtesy of a duskhorde attack—gave him an appearance some found shocking. "I would love to raise a fledgling or two." There was no denying the longing in his voice. His spine stiffened. "I doubt one will have me. Many will seek their attention. None will spare *me* a glance."

I grunted, unsure how to respond to that statement. As a warrior, few could compete with Durran. He was second only to his father in his clan, a position with considerable power. Ferlaern females would see his scars as proof of his ability to protect her and their young. Would Earthlings feel differently?

"Are you nervous about the melding tomorrow?" Durran asked, studying my face.

I kept my expression neutral. "Why should I be?"

"You've led your clan since your father's death, but he didn't grant you his powldron. Others try to take the leadership away from you."

Skydar, he meant, not *others*. Just one male fought each cycle to usurp me.

"I will trust fate in this," I said, keeping any hint of concern from my voice. "If the powldron doesn't choose me, so be it." While my father's decision to grant his powldron to me or take it to his grave was his to make, it still burned in my gut that he denied me this honor. "I was young when he died." Immature. I could hardly blame him for not granting his powldron to a male of only sixteen cycles. A family powldron assured succession. Him insisting on being buried with it left us floundering. Leaderless.

"You rose through the ranks and claimed leadership regardless," Durran said.

"I had no choice." The words left a bitter taint on my tongue.

He huffed. "There is always a choice."

"Not for me." I yanked my gaze from his perceptive one before he read my true thoughts. I did worry this recently discovered powldron wouldn't meld with me. How could I hold onto my leadership without one? I proved myself in combat each cycle, but our traditions had to be followed. Without a powldron, I was a leader, not a full warlord. Leaders were forced to fight for their right to rule each cycle. Warlords reigned until death.

However… A warlord was not allowed to form a maelstrom bond. If his second heart beat for one female, he must either spurn her or relinquish the powldron. A warlord could only mate to ensure his or her succession.

A flicker in the sky showed seven Ferlaern winging our way. The flap of wings resounded as the flight of trundiers approached. They circled overheard, their beasts shrieking challenges to ours who flicked out their wings and arched their spines.

We mounted our trundiers and lifted off. Veskar snapped and snarled at Skydar's beast, but a nudge of my heels made him back down. A winged battle would not impress the Earthlings.

Skydar nodded curtly, but his gaze was trained on the activity below us. "You did not approach," he stated with an edge of warning in his voice.

"Brother, please," a soft voice said from behind him. Skydar's sister, Meriwee, eased her mount higher than Skydar's. I've always enjoyed her company. She was a true friend, unlike Skydar. "You know Garek wouldn't go near them, not until we all arrived." He accused me of what he'd do himself, as was his way. Meriwee's soft purple gaze met mine, and her tail swept back and forth, brushing against the firm exoskeleton of her trundier. The siblings were complete opposites; Skydar grumpy and demanding, while Meriwee was kind and thoughtful, as if she felt the need to be twice the person her brother was to make up for where he lacked.

"Enough. We go," Skydar said, lifting his hand. His beast dove down, toward the valley.

Meriwee shook her head but took off after her brother, her lavender-streaked black hair streaming behind her.

We followed and as we drew close, the females scurried away from their partially erected canvas structures and clustered in the middle of the wide-open area.

Our trundier were the largest predators on Ferlaern, but the duskhorde rivaled them in a battle. We must be an intimidating sight, nine winged Ferlaern swooping down on them from above. We landed and dismounted, and as we approached, the females gasped. They stared with wide eyes, bumping together, sticks clutched in their hands.

Their heads barely reached my mid-chest, and I was of average height. And their body surface—it wasn't bronzed or segmented like a Ferlaern. Their smooth outer layer looked strange on a living being.

Skin, it was called, and it came in a variety of dusky colors. They had hair much like ours, though without the deep purple fire ours contained. No horns. No tusks. No tails. I sighed, unsure about this.

One of the females caught my eye. She had a curvy build I couldn't help noticing. My cock noticed, too, the unruly thing. Her hair rivaled the sunset, a mix of fiery red, gold, and the deepest amber. She'd pulled it up and a swatch dangled down her back in a glistening wave. A fledgling male stood in front of her like he thought she needed protection. His gaze met mine before darting to our trundiers. He eased away from the group as the female stepped toward me, her chin lifted and her spine tight.

The sway of her lush body stunned me. My mouth went dry, and my stupid cock twitched, the culier strands along the sides elongating and quivering. I shifted my pants and hoped my semi-erection wasn't obvious. What was wrong with me? We were here for introductions, not mating.

"I'm Piper," she said, holding out her hand. Her eyes—greener than the vetter desert—met mine. "I'm…I guess you could say I'm the current leader of our group until we hold a vote for mayor."

I did not know what a mayor was, but I understood the baring of her blunted teeth and her outstretched hand. Earth sent a protocol manual, and I studied it in anticipation of the females' arrival. The baring of teeth was a welcoming gesture. A hand extended was supposed to be shaken.

"Garek," I said. My fingers engulfed hers, and as I

rattled her hand, pumping it up and down to make sure I fully engaged it, she sucked in a breath.

Hell, I did, too. I caught her scent and it sunk into my skin. I found myself picturing her lying on my bed furs, completely naked, her hand extended in invitation.

Fuck. I needed to end that thought immediately.

She eased her fingers from mine and pressed them against her sides, her gaze flicking to the others as if for support.

"I'm the leader of the Suthen Clan," I said, nudging my head back. "Also with me are representatives of the three other clans in this region, the Willen, Nulet, and Osten clans, plus a few others." I introduced them one by one, though Meriwee hung back with her brother. "We welcome you to Ferlaern and hope you will be happy here." I wrenched my eyes from Piper's and scanned the rest of her group. Some stared at us blankly, others gulped and cringed. I hated that they appeared afraid. Didn't they know we would treasure them always? "Tomorrow, we'll start building your Earthlike village." Hearing our intentions should help them relax.

"About that," Piper said. She swallowed and her slender neck worked with the motion. I'd learned staring was wrong, but I couldn't help myself. Up close, she was...lovely. Appealing. So petite and lush. I wanted to lift her into my arms and stride around with her on my shoulder. "We have additional plans for the layout," she said in a rush.

"We're happy to do whatever you wish." Who

wanted to start a battle with the females before they got to know us? We'd gladly construct whatever they needed.

"See, that's the thing." Her spine stiffened and unease flashed across her face. "We want to do more than build regular houses. We want to create a new wild west with a central gathering place, a market, and a main street."

"What is this feral west?" I asked pleasantly.

She blinked slowly before her face cleared. "I can show you the drawings first thing tomorrow."

"That would be helpful." We were strong and brawny. We could construct whatever they wanted, even this…feral west.

"In between then, if you guys are able to give us a hand, could you help us set up our tents?" Her gaze scanned me and the others shuffling nearby. "We've got twenty-five mattresses to fill, as well. You guys are big."

"We are."

One of her auburn eyebrows lifted. "You look like you have decent lung volume."

I wasn't sure what she meant, but this must be a compliment. I dipped forward in a short bow, one worthy of the leader of the Earthling group. "We do have the decent volume. In all things."

"Yeah," she said with a twist of her lips. Lush and pink, how would they feel beneath mine? "The air mattresses will appreciate it."

The other males eased forward, as did Meriwee.

Seeing a female among us seemed to ease the

Earthlings' tension. Who could be frightened when Meriwee gave them her sunny smile? She went around the group, shaking hands, and I began to believe things would go smoothly from now on.

Until a yelp behind me was followed by a huffing grumble.

"Noah," Piper cried, leaping around me.

Her fledgling stood before Veskar, boldly reaching up to stroke the beast's snout. While completely tame with me, Veskar could be aggressive with strangers.

Piper flung herself between them, her teeth bared and a snarl ripping from her throat.

Veskar snorted and reared back, his black, brittle wings extending.

He dove toward Piper.

2

Piper

A giant hornet was going to bite my head off. Then it would eat my son, Noah.

I faced it with a snarl, a tight spine, and a rock. My chin was lifted, and my heart was aflame but inside, I was a wreck. Who wouldn't be? We were told Ferlaerns rode "mighty beasts of the sky," but we scoffed, assuming they meant a big bird, not something straight out of a nightmare.

Its outer hull was a deep, walnut brown, and it had long, brittle-appearing wings. Standing on four legs, the stinger on its butt poked forward, ready to impale me.

My pulse thundered. I spiraled my arms in the air like a freaked-out bird with guttural shrieks erupting from my throat.

The creature screeched and arched its spine, its poker jutting close enough, I sucked in my gut and stumbled backward. Its lips peeled back, revealing long, pointy teeth like arm-length spears.

This time, I would die protecting my son. So be it. I wasn't there for him when John hit him but I sure as hell was here for him now.

Noah clung to my waist; his wide eyes trained on the beast.

I lifted my rock, determined to get in one strike before it ripped me apart, but someone rushed between us, his arms lifted.

Garek spoke in a soothing voice that almost calmed me, too. But John spoke softly more often than not, only to show my judgment of men was completely off when his hand whipped out to strike.

While the warrior—*alien*—tugged the creature's head down and stroked its long snout, I pivoted, keeping a tight grip on Noah. I scooped him up and carried him ten feet or so away before dropping him to his feet and pushing him behind me. It wasn't easy to haul him even this far. He was big for eight. Seventy-two pounds at his last check-up. His final check-up on Earth. Who would measure his growth here?

"Mom," he complained, but I ignored him, grabbing onto his upper arm to hold him close as he wrangled to get away from me. When I half-barked, half-wailed at him, he stilled. He stared up at me, his face sagging as he took in the horror etched into my features.

My eyes stung with tears. Damn me for crying. My lungs raged; I couldn't calm down. I came all this distance to escape the trap we found ourselves in back on Earth only to almost lose my son within hours of our arrival.

Garek turned away from the beast, and I girded myself for it to bite him in two like it wanted to do with me. The beast dropped to its belly, whimpering like it begged the guy's forgiveness. It turned solemn eyes my way, but I wasn't buying it.

As Garek strode toward me, I backed a few steps, dragging my unruly son with me. Would he chastise me for not having better control over Noah?

He wore only dark pants molding his hips and thighs. A bulge pressed against the front of the material that couldn't be real because it was too big. His chest was exposed, other than crossing leather straps holding various weapons, reminiscent of a gladiator movie I watched once.

I straightened, preparing myself to be verbally whipped. That's what John did. My chin trembled, but I doubted anyone but me would know. I long ago learned to mask my emotions, to remain stoic no matter what was thrown my way.

He stopped in front of me, saying nothing, just staring down with his unreadable, deep green eyes. They were attractive eyes, something I couldn't believe I was noticing in a tense moment like this.

I tightened my spine and lifted my still-shaky chin, needing to tip my head back to look up at him. Damn, he was huge.

"I'm sorry." The words burst out of me, fed by my horror about what almost happened to my son, worry the creature would attack, and plain old fear of this alien. I shouldn't be scared of him. They welcomed us here. They asked us to settle. Had I blown it for everyone else? "Noah didn't mean to go near your…"

"Trundier," he offered in a low, husky voice that made my spine tingle.

"Yes, trundier." So that's what they were called. The literature they sent only contained vague mentions of protocols and terrain, not specific details about enormous, vicious creatures. When it mentioned the aliens, it was mostly braggy and I had to wonder who wrote it—him?

I could already see the description might not be all brag. They told us these guys were mighty warriors. Yeah, sure, I thought when I read that bit. But they were. Garek had to be seven-three or four. The literature mentioned their height, too, but who could picture something like that? I imagined a tall version of Conan the Barbarian and hooted with laughter because…they must be slender, little green men with ego issues, right? Big mistake on my part.

He was massively built, his broad shoulders the width of a blacksmith's, supported by a chest made up of rock-solid muscle. Not a skimp of fat on this male. Segmented, leather-like skin the color of a bronze statue coated every speck of his exposed torso. He was a bronze god, actually. His coloring didn't reflect the heavy beams of the setting sun, they glinted across him as if his external layer absorbed the rays and converted them into something divine. Black hair brushed across his shoulders, highlighted with dark purple bands as if the deepest, most magical night competed with his daylight skin.

I needed to stop staring. I needed to stop internally gushing about him.

"He wouldn't have touched your…trundier," I added, hating that my choked-off throat gave away my fear. *Never lower your guard. Always remain alert.* Words I chanted too many nights before I went to the police about John. I could take anything he dealt me but then he turned on our son.

"Veskar would not have harmed your fledgling." His low, grumbly voice shot through me like a lightning bolt. It made me stiffen in defense because I wanted him to sound unpleasant, not compelling. I had a wild feeling this male would play a major role in my life, and this disconcerted me.

My gaze shot to his again, and his lips curled slightly, inching up his tusks. I read about their tusks, too, but imagined something thick jutting down from their upper gum, much like a walrus. Instead, these were smaller, the thickness and length of my pinky and rooted in his lower jaw. They weren't as scary as I imagined. But his horns…

"That's good," I said, my body sagging.

I barely slept during the months leading up to our escape. Worry consumed me. John got out of jail and left a cryptic message on my phone: He was coming. He was mad. He would make me pay. I thought of going to the cops, but John had a way of getting what he wanted.

Eager to flee, I applied for the alien settlement

program, putting in a rush application that was thankfully accepted within days. I made it clear I wasn't looking for a true bride program like we were doing on the other alien planets. This meant I was selected for Ferlaern, the planet few Earthlings knew much about. They asked for settlers, not brides, though they welcomed relationships if the women were interested.

I thought my worries would be over once we reached this planet, but it was clear I had no clue about what I was getting into, and it wasn't just the environment. Garek intrigued me, something unexpected and unwelcome.

"I…" He shook his head, and his thick hair scattered across his ginormous shoulders. No, I did not wish to run my fingers through those strands. I huffed. As if this not-so-horrifying male would even deign to look at me, let alone permit me to touch him.

My face overheated. I didn't come here for me; I came to ensure Noah was safe for always. So much for that plan. Within hours of our arrival, he endangered his life. I needed to keep a closer eye on him.

Noah sidled around to stand beside me, staring up at the alien.

"You probably heard, but I am Garek," the big brawny guy said, holding his hand out to my son. That crushed my heart just a little. Few people bothered with kids, as if they blended into the woodwork and were to be ignored.

"Noah Cushing," my son said in a chirpy voice, latching onto one of Garek's thick fingers and giving it a shake. "Your hornet is awesome." He tilted his head. "Can I ride him?"

"Oh, Noah, that's not possible," I said. My gaze sought Garek's—brave of me considering how skittish I felt around him.

"Not tonight, youngling," Garek said in an indulgent tone. His sparkling green gaze met mine. "But surely tomorrow after our work is done."

Noah sidled closer to Garek. "You have horns and a tail. That's awesome."

Garek's tail twitched behind him, long and slender with a rounded, rubbery tip. It was as bronze as the rest of him. Was his entire body this color?

I squirmed at the boldness of my thoughts. "Please, Noah. It's not polite to talk about someone else's body parts. You know that."

"We're different, are we not?" Garek said cheerfully. He peered around to the back of Noah. "Where's your tail?" His fingers tapped Noah's temples. "Oh, no tail. And no horns." He sighed as if this was the saddest thing in the world.

"Will they grow, do you think?" Noah asked, his head tilting. "I want horns. A tail. Tusks like you." His burgeoning hero worship was sweet, but this male would not have time to indulge my son.

"Noah," I warned. "Please."

"They look awesome," Noah sighed. "And vicious."

"I have been known to be vicious in battle," Garek said. I swore he laughed but if so, he didn't give it away to my son. I appreciated that he didn't make

Noah's comment the butt of a joke. "I do not believe you will grow horns or a tail, fledgling." He braced his hand on Noah's shoulder kindly. "One can still be a brave warrior without them."

"Yes," Noah breathed, his attention fully absorbed in this brutish-appearing alien. "I'm gonna be a brave warrior, too, when I grow up." He leaped away from Garek to grab a stick he poked into the air. "I'll kill all the bad guys and hunt and fight battles. I'll be vicious, too."

"Know that a warrior must also be gentle." Garek's gaze drilled into mine, and I knew, just knew that his next words were for me. "Despite my tusks, I do not bite."

What if I wanted him to bite? I could picture his tusks gliding across my skin. His tongue… Shit. I needed to stop that train of thought right now.

"I'm glad to hear that," I said in a bright voice. "Should we get back to the others?" A glance over my shoulder showed the rest of the aliens mingling with my friends. A few kids darted around, squealing, though they remained far away from the trundiers. I hadn't expected to see a female Ferlaern among them, as I knew most died from the disease. Her gaze met mine, and I warmed to see her welcome. It would be nice to make new friends.

"I will help you set up your temporary structure if you wish," Garek said as I turned back to face him. "Then you will sleep snugly tonight."

"That's…nice of you." He seemed to be acting friendlier than I'd expect from one leader to another.

Should I tell him I wasn't in the market for a mate? Back on Earth, I felt impervious to anyone's charms. I thought it would be easy to focus on Noah and my new home without distractions from the males. Now…?

What would it be like if Garek wanted to court me? An old-fashioned term, but one they used in their literature. They promised to help us feel comfortable on this distant planet. Construct our town. Then they would seek our hands in marriage.

"Mine is on the end," I said, taking Noah's hand to lead him away from the beasts. "Stay away from the trundiers, Noah." If I knew my son, he'd find a way to sneak over to them again. "I mean it."

"Mom," he sighed, but he knew I meant business.

Garek followed us, and I could feel his gaze on my spine. It made me warm in places I shouldn't.

Who would've thought I'd be attracted to one of these aliens from the moment I met him?

As I wove through my friends and the aliens, aiming for my tent, I had to wonder.

If he expressed interest, could I trust Garek enough to let him into my life?

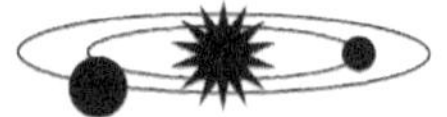

3

Garek

I was well and truly stunned. I never imagined I would be interested in any of these females. I convinced myself they were defenseless and puny. Unattractive.

Now heat roared through my veins, demanding I get down on one knee and beg this female—Piper—to allow me to be her mate.

I followed the tiny female, mesmerized by the soft sway of her hips. The fiery beams shooting from her hair in the setting sunlight drew the eye of every male in the encampment. Skydar, especially. He watched us with the look of a predator with prey. I wanted to snap at them all and tell them to look elsewhere, which was unbelievable. I didn't want her, did I?

Her flowery scent drifted through the air, sinking into my pores. If only I could trace her fine, smooth skin with my tongue. My tail whipped around, nipping at her delicate ankles. It was all I could do not to stroke her legs.

Fuck. I was well and truly fucked. I didn't have time for this. Wanting a female could be my downfall. It wasn't weak to wish for a mate, but this was why warlords were not allowed a maelstrom bond. If a warlord was distracted by a female, how could he put his clan first?

Piper led her son over to the other fledglings playing in the dust near the half-erected canvas structures. "Stay with the other kids, Noah. I mean it."

Like a trundier pup, I followed her to where she stopped to speak with the other females. She mingled, shaking hands with my clansmales. Only Skydar's gaze lingered on her in particular now that the males mixed among the females.

From the time we were young, he craved everything I had, from the weapon my grandsire gave me to the trundier pup I picked to tame. If he was wise, he would seek a different female for mating. He could sire a fledgling from any of the other females, not Piper.

She must've noticed his intent attention, as she darted him a flustered glance, and her face tightened. Stepping behind another female, she evaded his gaze.

I strode over to her, as drawn to her as a bizzire to a flower and stood between them. I was not staking a claim, though I wasn't completely sure what signal I was sending to Skydar other than leave Piper alone. Her look of relief sunk into me like a cool breeze on a humid day. It made my chest swell. My cock, too.

Skydar caught my eye, and I read his warning there. As if he could make his intentions clear with a female from a distance? None of them would be forced to court. We were expected to ask and if granted permission, *then* we could insinuate a claim to the other males.

My steely gaze did not drop away from his. Surely, he noted how I lingered beside her. It showed intentions.

Fuck. I had intentions?

Gnashing his tusks, Skydar walked over to Meriwee and spoke to her in a low voice.

"Which is your canvas structure?" I asked.

"The one near the end." She waved her hand in that direction.

"Once it is settled, I will prepare a welcome feast in your honor."

The pink of a new dawn rose into her face, and she dragged her gaze from mine. "That's very nice of you." Her attention went to her son. "Noah, stay nearby, please. Do not go near the trundiers."

"Aw, mom…" he moaned, his face a mass of disappointment.

"I could take him flying tomorrow," I said, feeling more excited about the prospect than I should. I had other plans for tomorrow. The ceremony at dawn. Accepting whatever came from it after that. Constructing the village as quickly as possible so I could return to my clan and assume permanent leadership. Hunting. There was no time to take a fledgling flying. Nor should I assist a surprisingly appealing Earthling female set up her temporary home but here I was, following her wherever she led.

It meant nothing. I wanted her safe. I worried

about all the females, I told myself. There was no other reason.

She nibbled on her lower lip, and I could not wrench my gaze away. Her lips were thin. As pink as her face, though that appeared temporary as the color arrived and retreated in waves. I could not discern the cause of the color, however. She was not exerting herself, something that occasionally made my skin darken.

These Earthlings were a puzzle I never thought I was eager to figure out.

"Let's wait to talk about Noah flying until tomorrow, okay?" she finally said. Her face softened as she watched her fledgling race and laugh with the others. "I know I'm a helicopter mom. I can't help it. I love my son very much. I'd do anything to see him happy. And after what happened…" Her face closed off with a snap.

"After *what* happened?" I wouldn't prod her to speak, but something in her voice… The deadened tone brought out all my protective instincts. Relief softened my breastplates. That's what this was. I was eager to protect the new settlers. This had nothing to do with her specifically.

"Let's just say I'm glad I left Earth. That we…got away."

"Someone tried to harm you?" Anger rumbled inside me; a dark cloud ready to drench the world.

More dew-kissed pink rose into her cheeks. "I really don't wish to discuss this. I hope that's okay."

"It is."

As I waved for her to lead me to her structure, I made a silent vow. I wouldn't press her to share, though something deep inside me ached to know what caused the pain in her voice and the fear on her face.

She strode to one of the sagging tents. A rueful laugh skipped from her, and I paused, listening as one did when a rare bird called in the wood.

"I really did take classes before coming here," she said. "I even erected this tent in my backyard a couple of times. Somehow, it was easier then. Maybe because Betty, my elderly neighbor, came over to help." She flicked the side of the structure and it leaned away from her. "Look at it. At this rate, we'll sleep beneath the stars, something Noah would enjoy but not me." Her arms snaked around her waist, and she peered into the dense woods as if fearing something big would attack. "We won't make it a week here if we don't get this show on the road."

Show on the…?

"I'll help," I said with a shake of my head. "*We* wish to help."

Like a newborn trundier, she was skittish. Wary. All I could do was show her she could trust me. A burden I welcomed, strangely enough.

At first glance, she seemed fragile, like a stiff wind could break her. But a core of strength shone in her eyes. This female had confronted my trundier. To protect her youngling, yes, but she didn't hesitate. She was as strong as any male in my clan. I ignored my eagerness to remain by her side until I understood all her expressions, everything that made up the inner strength of this gentle female.

Until I unlocked the puzzle of *her*.

4

Piper

Garek was something else. Big and brawny as I already noted, but he had a gentle side he seemed hesitant to share. It came through when he interacted with Noah and when he helped me fix my tent.

We hadn't planned to ask them for help beyond constructing our town. That was enough. Everyone pitched in, and soon our tents stood in a neat circle, looking cozy. Welcoming. Like a home, even if they were only temporary.

The males gathered wood from the nearby forest, dragging out entire stumps I wouldn't be able to lift, let alone carry. Garek hoisted two onto his shoulders and strode to the center of our tent structures and laid them down with a bang. Noah galloped along beside him with kid-sized branches clutched in his hands, chattering away. I appreciated his patience with my son, but I worried Noah would be irritating. But when

Garek looked my way, his eyes sparkled, leading me to believe he actually enjoyed spending time with Noah.

Perhaps it would be good to include some of these males in our lives.

John was convicted three years ago and sent to jail. Noah missed him at first but lately, he seemed to have forgotten his father, like he was a chapter we finished and turned the page to start another. Seeing him eager to interact with Garek made me realize he needed more than just me to be happy. I rubbed my chest where it hurt but gave him a smile when he looked my way.

"These guys are hotter than I anticipated," Rayne said, fanning her face. She shifted her sneakers beside me, tamping down the deep blue grass. "I see you've caught the attention of one of them already. The head of the group even. You go, girl."

"He's not paying me any more attention than the rest of the group." Liar. Garek watched me.

He was kind and sweet and I hated to nudge him away, but I couldn't offer whatever he might seek.

Rayne chuckled but she kept it low. "During the trip here, you were one of the few who didn't gush about meeting new guys. I wondered but didn't ask."

And I wasn't eager to share my past any more now than while traveling, but we were friends. Four of us drawn together, perhaps because we were all single moms.

My gaze met Alexa's. She had her hands full with her two-year-old twin boys, but I noticed one of the aliens lingering nearby as if he wanted to offer assistance but didn't dare. Josie, our nurse, had a thirteen-year-old daughter who was super sweet. Both of them worked on their tent with two of the aliens assisting.

"I left Earth because I had to," I told Rayne in a low voice like I worried voicing even this bit of information could draw John's evil gaze my way.

Garek stood beside Noah, talking with one of the other males. His eyes met mine, and I wondered if he could hear us speaking. He must be too far away, and Noah's chatter would almost drown out a marching band.

"What did you run from?" Rayne asked softly. "Or should I say who?"

"My ex. He… He hurt me and I put up with it. But when he turned to Noah, I couldn't do it anymore. You know what I mean?"

She placed a caring hand on my arm. "I'm sorry. That must've been rough."

"It was, but we're here now. He can't hurt us any longer. We'll make a new life in our new wild west. You don't know how much I've looked forward to this. I'll raise Noah and live in peace."

"You'll have a hard time trusting someone new, but…"

"But what?"

Her smile was kind and encouraging. "Give this world—these guys—a chance?"

"I haven't been here long enough to commit to something like that."

"I get it. But don't close yourself off."

It sounded like she spoke from experience, though she hadn't indicated she came from an abusive situation like me.

"I'll keep an open mind," I said. Not really. The thought of being with someone else, of letting him into my life, was scary.

She gave me a quick hug. "Perfect. Now why don't you go help Garek haul some logs?"

I snorted. "I can't carry anything like that."

"No need to. Just be with him. Get to know him. He seems sweet."

"Sweet for sure, but he's huge."

"Sweet things can come in big packages, amirite?"

"Like what?"

She chuckled. "I don't know. Maybe one of these big old cinnamon bun guys."

"You're suggesting Garek is a cinnamon bun?"

Her chestnut brown eyebrows wiggled. "Why don't you dip your finger into his icing and taste him?"

I slapped her arm but laughed along with her. "You."

"It's okay to be afraid, but sometimes, it's also okay to hold your hand out to someone special." She gave me a squeeze. "Just remember that."

"I will," I said with a sigh.

For the first time in too long, I was tempted. I couldn't believe I wanted to feel close to someone. Not just someone. Garek.

So strange. I never intended anything like this, but feelings were creeping up on me slowly. "I… I won't make any decisions about this without thinking it through first."

"Okay, then." She nudged my spine, urging me toward Garek, who was striding toward the woods again with Noah panting along beside him like a puppy. "Go help."

She chuckled as I scooted in the guys' direction.

"You can't do this, Mom," Noah said, puffing his tiny chest when I caught up to them. "Hauling wood is a male's job."

"Who says?" I asked with a teasing poke to his arm.

He peered up at Garek, seeking support. "Garek is strong. He could tear down two trees at the same time and carry them like they were sticks, right Garek?"

"Not two, fledgling," Garek said in an indulgent tone. "Perhaps only one." His gaze met mine, sharing the joke with me.

"Maybe I could tear down a tree and haul it around myself," I said.

Noah snorted. He darted ahead of us, gathering sticks as he ran. "This is kindlin'. Garek says we need lots of kindlin' and it's my job as a fledgling to collect it."

"Thank you," I said softly as Noah skipped to a clump of sticks on the ground ahead of us.

"For what?"

"For being patient with him. I know kids can nag at times, and I appreciate that you're not brushing him off."

"Brushing…" He frowned, the plates on his forehead crunching together. "Ah, yes, like one would with a fleser, brushing it away before it lands for a bite."

A fleser must be some kind of fly or mosquito. "Noah is, to use his favorite word, awesome, but even I reach the limits of my patience with him on occasion." My heart glowed with pride, though I didn't have much to do with it. I birthed him, but he came out with his bubbly personality fully intact. "He's a good kid." There wasn't anything I wouldn't do to ensure he was happy.

Garek's face sobered. "Many of our young died from the disease, not only our females."

"I'm sorry." We lost men but almost no children. "For us, it happened almost three years ago as the disease slowly worked its way through the galaxy."

"Here…" His gaze scanned the forest as if seeking potential threats. It made my heart skip, but it also made me feel secure. Safe for the first time in forever. "The plague swept across Ferlaern almost ten cycles ago. The few surviving younglings have grown. We're an empty, mourning race."

"I'm sorry," I said again. I wanted to offer more than just the comfort of words, but I had nothing else.

"There's nothing to be sorry about. Your arrival has brought hope to Ferlaern."

"Most of the women are eager to meet the males of your clan. I'm sure things will work out for them."

"And for yourself?" His tight scrutiny made my steps falter. "Do you hope to meet the males of my clan?"

"I don't know if I'm…" I couldn't say it. I sucked

in a deep breath and released it. "For now, I want to build my home. And a barn! We have grand plans for a large central community building where we can gather and have fun. Potluck dinners. Karaoke night. Even old-fashioned square dancing. But as for meeting someone, I'm not sure if or when I'll be ready for something like that. I'm sorry if you, um…" Jeez, don't say it. Maybe he wasn't indicating interest. He could be carrying on a simple conversation.

He reached out slowly like he was worried I'd draw away from his touch. His big fingers gently glided the hair off my face, tucking it behind my ear. "There is no need to say anything more. I am here. You are here. And that is all this is."

Such a lighthearted way of looking at it. I loved the lack of pressure.

"Let us gather more wood and then we will cook our feast. That is all we need to do this munette." He bent down near a huge log and hefted it over his shoulder like it was a twig. It was enough firewood to burn for three days.

"We brought equipment to cut and split the wood," I offered, picking up a few random sticks. Maybe it was my job as Noah's mom to pick up kindlin' after all. "Plenty of axes."

"This is good. We'll cut some when we return to your encampment."

When we got back and unloaded our wood, he directed some of his males, asking them to cut and split it in anticipation of the fire. The rest of us were sent to collect rocks. Noah couldn't carry anything heavy, but he put his back into it, doing what his idol asked without a single complaint. Back home he balked at anything resembling chores.

"I must leave but I will not be gone long," Garek said to me as I dropped my rocks in the central area and brushed my hands off on my jeans.

"All right."

Pivoting, he left.

While I should be helping my friends build our firepit, I watched Garek instead as he walked to his trundier. He had a nice ass. I shouldn't be noticing that if I wasn't interested, right? I liked his firm, purposeful stride, too. He didn't swagger or act cocky, though he could. He had everything going for him, from his looks to his position as leader of his clan.

With one bound, he leaped onto the trundier's back. They flew up and reared around, soaring toward the mountains. I stared after them for far too long.

"I get it," Rayne said with a gleeful elbow-nudge to my side. "I can't keep from watching one or two of these guys myself. But it's time to get back to work." She winked.

I rolled my eyes and followed her to the rock pile. We placed them in a circle then spread dirt in a thick layer in the center. In no time, a merry fire crackled, sending sparks into the air like alien fireflies.

The sun was sucked down below the horizon, and a chill set in, gliding out from the forest. From what I read; this was the normal temperature for early spring on Ferlaern. In the summer, we'd see about eighty degrees during the day and the fifties at night. In the spring and fall, it was cooler, and snow fell here in the winter, though it didn't stick, like in southern New England, where I lived back on Earth.

I shivered when I realized how little time we had to get ready for the long, cold months. Our solar panels would generate electricity for our homes, but most of our heat would come from firewood.

"Next, we'll craft a feast," Garek said from behind me.

My heart skipped a beat. How had I missed his return?

Turning, I kept my face neutral.

He hefted a slab of meat the size of half a cow.

"Where did that come from?" I asked, my voice thready. It wasn't because he came back, or he was near. Or because he smelled good, like an unusual spice. And it sure wasn't because his face reflected caution like he knew I was as timid as a deer about to bolt into the woods.

"Garek," Noah cried, rushing over to us. "Holy…" he said in awe as he stared at the hunk of meat. "That's a big, honking bloody thing." Instead of gulping or backing away, his hands fidgeted as if he wanted to help Garek carry the carcass.

"We hunted earlier and stored it in the hills," he said.

"How?" One more thing I needed to learn. While I might not be able to bring down something this size,

I learned how to set snares to trap creatures the size of rabbits. I would spread them out in the woods tomorrow.

"How did I hunt?" he asked. "Veskar did most of the work." When he flashed his tusks, warmth flooded me. "As for storing it, there are caves in the mountains that are cold during all seasons. In my domit valley, we maintain closed off compartments where we leave meat for a brief time. We crafted a compartment for you in the mountains. We'll show it to you soon."

"That's amazing."

"Didn't you have a way to keep meat fresh on Earth?"

"We do."

"I'll soon have it cooking over the fire," he said, striding around me. He paused, looking back at me over his shoulder. "Would you like to help?"

My gaze shot to Noah, who'd drifted away and now knelt with the other kids, driving metal cars around in the dirt.

"Sure," I said, following Garek.

He took the meat to the river and washed it. I took the opportunity to scrub my hands.

After returning to the fire pit, he handed me the huge hunk of meat.

It weighed me down, though it was lighter than Noah. I held in my sputter and stared down at it as he strode away. Somehow, it was easier to eat meat when it came in tiny packages. But this was our new wild west, right? I needed to adjust and adjusting meant hunting, cleaning whatever I caught, and cooking it over a fire until our wood stoves were installed.

The other women worked on their tents or continued to help with the wood the guys were splitting. I wanted to call Rayne over so she could stand with me. Not to help hold the meat but… Okay, to be a buffer between me and Garek. He disconcerted me. Made me want things I shouldn't be considering.

Here for Noah. Here for Noah, I chanted under my breath.

But… Was it wrong to also be here, just a tiny bit, for me?

He strode beyond the tents and proceeded to roll a boulder the size of a refrigerator close to the fire. After washing his hands in the river and dousing the rock with a bucket of water, swirling his palm across the surface to clean it, he took the meat from me with another flash of his tusks.

More tingles erupted inside me.

He laid the meat on the boulder and proceeded to cut it into manageable chunks that more closely resembled what I saw in the supermarket.

The burly woodcutter aliens finished stacking the last of the wood and went to the river to clean up. Most of the women followed—pretty much fluttering, but I could see why. These guys were kind, strong, and incredibly sexy.

Their laughter rang out as they dug long tubers from the bank together. After shaving off the outer layer, they cut them into chunks and placed them in bags impervious to fire.

The women trailing them like a fan club and watched while the guys suspended the bags on sticks propped over the coals. A nutty, savory aroma soon filled the air and made my stomach growl.

Once Garek finished cutting the meat, we threaded the chunks on sticks like shish kababs.

"I hear your belly protesting," Garek said with a smile. "You are hungry and soon, I'll feed you."

His comment came out sexy because his eyes seemed to gleam only for me.

"We packed protein bars, but we'll save them for a time when we can't find other food," I said lamely. Like I'd pull one out and offer it after seeing what they planned to feed us tonight?

"Meat, fruit, and vegetables are plentiful in this region. You will never want for anything."

Except a warm body next to mine.

Now where had that though come from? Just because he was kind and helpful and too attractive for his own damn good, didn't mean I had any interest in luring him between my sheets.

"We'll learn to dry food and can it," I said. "We brought equipment and instruction manuals."

"I could teach you everything you need to know about surviving in my world," he offered. His gaze didn't meet mine, but I got the idea he intently awaited my answer.

"Oh, um…" I leaned into his side, ready to say something that didn't sound too flirty. Something that would show I might—and that was a BIG might—be slightly interested in hanging out with him.

Actually I really did want to hang out with him.

He gazed down at me, his face sobering. I got this strange feeling he was going to kiss me. His head lowered. I rose onto my tiptoes.

One of the kids screamed.

5

Garek

I spun away from Piper and rushed toward the river, where the scream came from.

Piper ran behind me.

"What's happening?" I asked Noah, when peering around didn't show me the cause. No threat approached from the woods or sky. A few of the fledglings stood on the riverbank but none appeared injured.

"It's Missy," he said, his eyes full of tears. He ran to his mother and clung to her side. "Missy fell into the water. Something grabbed her, and now she's gone!"

I whipped my head in that direction, studying the water for movement. "Which direction?"

He pointed. "That way."

"Missy?" one of the women wailed. "Missy!"

Piper's horrified gaze met mine.

I shucked my chest straps and pants while I half-ran toward the river, wearing only the thin scrap of cloth I wore beneath. Time was limited. I had to save the precious youngling.

I dove into the water and sought her, swimming with the current while studying the bottom of the channel. Barbids hunted these waters. I thought the females would be wary but perhaps they were unaware of the threat. From what I read; Earth had few predators. We would sit down with them after the younglings slept and explain the dangers of this world.

Ahead, I spied the struggle. The barbid was nearly the size of the fledgling, and its teeth were locked onto her thigh. She twisted, straining to reach the surface as I rushed in that direction.

I grabbed the barbid by the snout and pried its jaws open, releasing the child. She flailed for the surface. I held the barbid back until she was free, then socked it hard enough in the snout to stun it. It sunk to the bottom and drifted across the mud. It would wake, but we would be long gone before it could seek revenge.

Swimming to the surface, I caught up with the youngling female who sobbed and made for the shore. Her mother waited on the bank, but when she spied us coming her way, she waded into the water, crying her child's name. She scooped her up and carried her to the shore where she lowered her to the grass. Her hands fluttered when she caught sight of the blood streaming down the fledgling's leg.

"Missy. No! Help. Help!"

"I'm here," a dark-haired woman said, rushing from one of the tents and toward the shore. She carried a black bag and when she reached the child, she dropped down beside her. Her hand stroked the girl's forehead. "It's going to be okay, Missy. I'll patch you up and you'll be as good as new. I promise."

"It hurts," the small child cried. "Mommy, the big fish grabbed me! I wanted to go swimming and the fish came after me."

"You know you can't go into the water without an adult around," her mother exclaimed, fear and tension heightening her voice. "Please, Josie. Tell me my little girl's going to be okay."

"She is," Josie said, cleansing the wound with a square of white material. "The bite didn't break the skin." She lifted the white square. "See? No need even for antibiotics."

I strode up the shore while the other women gathered around the child. Water sluiced down my body.

Noah ran up to me, holding out my pants. "Man, you're so gonna get into trouble. Get dressed fast before Mom sees you're not wearin' much of anything. Holy," his eyes widened, "you're not wearin' boxers."

"What are boxers?"

"Aww," Noah said, staring up at me with his jaw unhinged. "Are you sayin' you never hafta wear boxers?" He spun away from me while I shook the dirt off my pants. "Mom. Mom! Garek doesn't wear boxers. How come I have to?"

My gaze caught Pipers', and that delightful color rose into her face. She took me in—all of me—and my cock twitched, the culier strands extending and humming.

Her hands fluttered but her eyes boldly met mine.

One thing was clear. She might fear many things on Ferlaern, but she did not fear me.

I could tell myself over and over I had plans for my future.

Bonding with a powldron.

Solidifying my warlord status with my clan.

Driving back the duskhorde.

But when I looked at Piper, all I could think about was mating.

6

Piper

I couldn't forget the image of Garek striding from the water nearly naked. The scrap of material covering his sizeable package kept flashing through my mind, though my lust was totally out of place considering the situation. It wasn't easy turning away from him to focus on the others.

Thankfully, Missy was okay. But the creature's attack shook all of us. It reminded us we were in a new, strange world with many unknown dangers. We were stupid to think this place was all sunshine and sweet grasses. One look at the trundier told me large predators hunted this land. Were some bigger than the giant hornets?

I sat with Rayne, eating.

"Look at them," I said, waving to the kids dancing around the fire, playing hide and seek near their tents, squealing until they were exhausted. "We're a wreck, and they're acting like it never happened."

"Except Savvy."

Josie's thirteen-year-old daughter herded the other four children back in this direction, though it was like wrangling puppies. She handed one of the two-year-old twin boys to Alexa then settled on the ground with the other on her lap. The child was soon fast asleep, his head pressed against her chest, his mouth half open.

"And them," Rayne nudged her head to a few of the women flirting with Ferlaerns.

Garek sat opposite us. Thankfully, he was dressed, though that didn't stop my imagination from spinning in all kinds of wild circles. He emerged from the water like a Greek god, all burnished skin, muscles, his enormous cock molded by the wet material. Size did not matter, I told myself. It was what you did with it that made all the difference, I added.

But, damn, all I could picture was him climbing over me and placing the head of his thick length at my entrance. I was wetter than I've been in my life, all from my stupid imagination.

His brooding gaze watched me, though it wasn't heavy or scary. It kept my skin aflame and my clit throbbing.

Dragging my gaze from his, I focused on my meal.

"This stuff isn't half bad," Rayne said, waving a hunk of the meat in the air.

"It's all fantastic," I said. The tubers had a salty, garlicy flavor and the texture of boiled potatoes. All in all, it was a satisfying first meal on Ferlaern. I was grateful we didn't have to dig into our reserves.

Missy and Noah joined us, leaning against our sides and stifling yawns.

It had been a long, stressful day. Our ship sent us down by shuttle. The crew unloaded supplies, waved, and left. We worked to sort through it and set up our tents. No wonder everyone was worn out.

"Never thought I'd live in a place with two moons," Rayne said, nudging her head to where they shone above us, one waxing, the other waning. Their light barely competed with the fire.

Composite building materials were stacked all over the place, and it would take days to sort through them. Our first priorities should be planting gardens and setting up a fenced area for the little kids to safely play in, but construction of our homes needed to be started first thing tomorrow. We needed doors we could shut tight at night. Windows. Hard walls and roofs overhead.

Maybe that was why we clung to our new wild west plan. Houses, a street, and a community center would make us feel like we were home even though the world around us was completely different.

A shadow passed over me, though it was only a sensation and not a living being swooping low. When I tipped my head back and looked around, I saw nothing. The shadow crossing my soul suggested a rough road was coming. So many things to do and not enough time to get to them. We were forging new territory.

My gaze met Garek's and the warmth I found there lit something inside me. I couldn't look away, not until his eyes left mine and narrowed on one of the other males. This guy watched me, too, but the heat in his gaze made me cringe. Meriwee sat with him. When she caught him staring, she nudged his thigh. I liked that she made an effort to keep him in line. It spoke well of her. Too bad he needed the tight rein.

"I'm going to put her to bed," Rayne said, kissing Missy's forehead. Her daughter slept, leaning against her mom's shoulder. "See you in the a.m." She rose and carried Missy toward her tent.

Noah slumbered, his head on my lap, and I stroked his soft hair, aiming for distraction.

Garek watched us but only kindness shone in his eyes.

After John, I went out of my way to send the *not available* signal. I couldn't trust my heart or my body to someone new and wouldn't allow anyone into my son's life unless they were fully vetted. Now I wondered if I dared trust Garek. Exhausted and sleepy, tomorrow was soon enough to contemplate a decision like that. We met, he was helpful, and I liked him. We were becoming friends. *Just* friends for now.

My low chuckle shot from me. Sure, just friends.

If that were the case, I wouldn't be fanaticizing about his cock.

7

Garek

I got up and fed the fire, but instead of returning to my spot opposite Piper, I joined her and her son.

Her fingers stroked Noah's hair, and she didn't look up.

"He's happy here," I said to break the silence.

"I think he will be. What happened with Missy was scary but perhaps a strong lesson for all the children." Her gaze lifted but was directed to the fire. "There are dangerous creatures on Earth. Poisonous snakes and spiders, and wild animals that sometimes attack, though they mostly avoid humans. This place looks and feels like paradise, but we need to remember there are dangers here just like there are back on Earth."

"We will protect you." *I* will protect *you*, though I did not say this.

"How?" She tipped her head back to look up at me, and when the flickering firelight gleamed on her face, I was reminded again of how lovely she was. "You won't be here for long. You'll help us build our homes, and we greatly appreciate that, but once you leave, we're kind of on our own, aren't we?"

"We will conduct regular patrols of the area from our trundier."

"Are your homes near here?"

"A few sunslice's flight away."

"Days?" She sighed. "I'm beginning to think it might be a mistake to build here instead of closer to your home."

"Settling in this valley was an Earth requirement."

"Why do you think they didn't want us moving to wherever you live?"

I shrugged, not privy to the decisions Earth made with our elders.

"It doesn't matter, I suppose," she said. "It's pretty here. Once our houses are built, I'm sure we'll find a way to fit in."

"Males will flock to females."

She grunted. "I assumed so, and for most of them, that will be welcome."

There it was again, her implication she wasn't interested in pursuing mating. Why come here then?

"Your trundiers are impressive," she said. "I appreciate the care and training you gave yours. He responded like a somewhat tame beast when presented with a challenge—my son and me."

"Veskar would not have harmed you or your fledgling."

"Well… It sure didn't seem that way to me."

Her low chuckled stirred me, and my cock twitched. What was it about this female? She was lovely as I already noted, but so were the others. They were all beautiful in their own way. Why did Piper ignite me like no one had before? Even when our females were still alive, I had not been drawn to any of them. I would have mated eventually as I wanted the comfort of a willing female in my bed furs. I also wanted younglings, but I had not felt as driven to mate as I did now with Piper.

"Veskar did nearly bite my head off," she said with a low laugh that glided down my spine.

I scoffed. "He might've nudged you away, but he wouldn't bite you."

"I'm glad you think so."

She didn't sound sure. I'd introduce her to Veskar again tomorrow and show her how gentle he could be.

"Tell me more about trundiers? I'm very curious."

"We share their eyrie with them."

"Whoa." She frowned. "You live with them? Like, um, sleep with them?"

I chuckled. "They have their own nests, as do we. We work with them from the time they hatch until they are ready to bond with a warrior."

"Bond? Like… Well, I'm not really sure what you mean by bond. Back home, though, we adopt kittens, puppies, and other assorted pets, so maybe it's kind of the same thing only on a…giant hornet scale."

"I am sure your kee-tens and poopies are the same thing. I hadn't heard you have flying beasts like a trundier on Earth, however."

"Now, we don't," she said with another soft

laugh. "Our, um, poopies don't fly. Nor do the kittens." She snickered, and I knew I mispronounced the words.

"What did I say?" I asked.

She laid her hand on my arm, and heat spread across my skin plates. "Poopies are, well, when we use the toilet, we generate something like that."

"Ah, shit."

"To put it bluntly, yes." She snickered, and I grinned along with her. Did she realize how she disarmed me? She made me ache in a way I never had before. She made me want more.

"There are large birds on Earth, though they're nowhere near the size of trundiers. And kittens and puppies are small." She held her hands an arm's length apart. "Even fully grown, most don't get bigger than this."

I frowned. "Then what use are they? Our trundiers carry us from one hunting ground to another and they drive prey toward us."

"Cats and dogs are pets. We pat them and play with them."

"I see." Although, I didn't. Not truly. "Why raise beasts that cannot be used for hunting or protection?"

"They can be; dogs anyway. They're quite loyal and they make a lot of noise if they think we're threatened. Cats...not so much, though they can be very loving. A dog is a grown puppy, and a cat is a grown kitten. We get them when they're young and train them."

"Like we do with trundiers, then."

Her lips twitched upward. "Yes. It's mostly the same thing."

"Did you have a kee-ten or poopie?" I grimaced. "Why can't I pronounce these words?"

"It's okay. It's kind of cute."

She thought I was cute? Or did she think the odd way I said her words was cute? If only I knew.

Her face fell. "We had a cat a while ago, but he was hit by a car. I miss him. He was the best boy ever."

"Perhaps you could adopt a trundier hatchling to replace this cat in your heart." Then she could see the wonders of Ferlaern from the sky. It would be difficult moving to a strange planet to start a new life. If she bonded with something from our world, the transition would be easier.

"Maybe." Her head tilted. "Are they cuddly when they're little?" Her fingers filtered through her youngling's hair.

"I cannot imagine cuddling them, but Veskar does enjoy it when I stroke his snout."

"Almost the same thing, then. Maybe..." She glanced around. "Maybe there's a creature here like a cat?"

"I don't know." I perked up at the thought of helping her find comfort here. "I'll seek one for you if you want."

"That's sweet of you." Her full smile bloomed, and my heart stilled. This female...

Why her?

Her head tipped forward, and she looked up at me

through her long lashes. "Let me get settled, and I might just take you up on that offer."

Stunned all over again by a simple gesture, I could only nod.

"As for Earth creatures that might be similar to trundiers, we raise horses, which are a fraction of the size and wingless," she said. "We ride on their backs, though. I'm not sure it's quite the same thing." Her gaze sought the trundiers resting close enough to watch but not so far that we couldn't reach them if needed. "They're amazing as long as they stay there while I'm over here. I can see why you make the effort to tame them, though. When you flew in," she shook her head, and her hair brushed across her shoulder, "it was magnificent."

My chest expanded at the thought of her admiring us—me. "We hunt with them, battle with them. They are an integral part of our clan."

"They aren't tied yet they remain where you left them. Some even sleep. They're truly domesticated like a cat or dog."

"Mostly," I said. "At all times, we must remember they're wild creatures first, our friends second. I trust Veskar but I'm cautious around the others."

"Yet you offered to let Noah ride Veskar tomorrow. I can't let him fly by himself."

"I would never do this. He'll ride with me. It would be a short flight, a circle around the valley before returning safely to your arms."

She nibbled on her lower lip, drawing my attention to her mouth. I wanted to taste her lips, run my tongue across them then part the seam and seek everything inside.

"You mentioned living in an eyrie?" she asked.

"Our homes have been among the trundier for as long as anyone can remember."

"Eyrie implies," a frown filled her face, "high in the sky?"

"A bit."

"Huh. I don't believe I've heard much about your homes."

Noah shifted and twitched.

"I guess I should get him to bed. A real bed, that is, and not my lap." She rolled her eyes. "Assuming I can move my legs after he's been lying on them so long. I think they went to sleep."

"Can I help? I could carry him to your tent for you."

"That would be great," she said softly. "He's still my baby. He'll still be my baby even when he's fully grown. But he's getting heavy. I'm not sure he could walk, and I hate to wake him."

I lifted the boy who was lighter than solarn dander and waited while she stood with a soft groan. It was followed by another smile as if we shared this munette.

My heart surged. Everything inside me surged. So did my cock, but it was an unruly thing, and it would have to behave for now.

For now? Fuck. Was I truly contemplating pursuing Piper for mating?

I needed to think, something that was impossible

when she was around. She confused me and made me long for a future I never envisioned.

I followed her to her tent. At the entrance, she tugged the silver fastener open, such an odd device I needed to look at further in the light of day. When she stepped inside, I followed, ducking low so I didn't smack my head against the ceiling. I took great care not to jostle Noah and laid him on one of the two mattresses. The fledgling did not stir. A blanket lay folded on the end of the bed, and I shook it out and laid it over him. Watched him. He was sweet when he slept and for the first time, I wondered what it would be like to have younglings running around my domit. Children to carry to bed after a long day's play. Sons like Noah.

"He should do his teeth," she whispered from beside me. She rubbed her son's back, and he settled, his breathing evening out as he drifted into deeper slumber. "I hate to wake him."

"Do what to his teeth?" I straightened as much as possible with the low ceiling and took care not to show my curiosity about her belongings. My gaze was drawn to her bed. I shouldn't be picturing us lying there together. It was small; my feet would stick off the end. And narrow. She would have to lie on top of me or we would tumble off the side.

But if she offered…

Shaking my head at my foolish notion, I followed her back out of the tent. She tugged the two sides of the door together but did not use the device to close it fully.

"Thank you," she said. Her eyes flicked up to mine before she took a step back like our closeness made her as uncomfortable as it did me.

I could not control my cock. Whenever she was near—when her scent filled my senses—I went rigid. Time to jump into the river again. Maybe if I wrangled with a barbid, I'd be distracted enough to forget how much I wanted this sweet female in my bed furs.

"I'll see you tomorrow?" she asked.

It would be wrong of me to read hope in her voice.

"I'll be here. Before we begin the construction of your…new feral west, I must attend a gathering in the mountains with some of the others but then we will wing down here and get started."

She shot a glance at the piles of building materials. "How long do you think it'll take to build our town?"

"Many suns."

Her eyes gleamed, reflecting the fire. "You've done this before?"

No, but we studied their designs. They were unlike our own, naturally occurring homes but the design wasn't highly complex.

"You shall see." I flashed my tusks. "We work quickly."

"So before fall?"

"Yes."

"Perfect." She edged around me and grabbed one side of the entrance flap. "Thank you again."

I dipped forward in a half bow. "You are welcome. Until tomorrow, Piper."

"Yes, tomorrow." She ducked inside and closed the entrance completely.

Rather than join my friends at the fire, I headed for the river.

Time to cool down and find a way to forget about this tempting female.

8

Piper

I woke to the long, deep shriek unlike anything I've heard before in my life.

When it ripped through the air again, I bolted upright on my bed. A glance at Noah showed he slept still, but that boy could sleep through the destruction of a building.

Repetitive thuds were followed by more shrieks.

In the woods.

Coming closer.

A guttural cry came from the direction of the trundiers. It was followed by the flapping of agitated wings. Were the sounds coming from them?

Another shriek made goosebumps lift on my skin. No, the cry was coming from the forest.

My heart leaped into my throat. I pushed aside my blankets and shoved my feet into my ankle-high boots, stuffing the laces inside the top rather than take time to tie them. I hurried to the tent flap and unzipped it, then slipped outside and tugged the two sections together to keep the bugs out.

Only coals smoldered in the firepit. Everyone must still be asleep.

Stomping drew my attention to the trundiers. On their feet, they stared in one direction, their glowing golden eyes sending chills up my spine. The head of one snapped around, in my direction. They were on our side—well, the Ferlaern's side—but my skin quivered with fear.

With a gulp, I stepped away from my tent. A big part of me wanted to duck back inside. Hide. But I stopped hiding when John hit my son. The cowering woman was gone, replaced by one with a backbone of steel.

I stepped forward and nearly smacked into Garek. His hands went around my waist to steady me, and his warmth sunk through my thin cotton nightgown.

He shifted me around behind him. "Wait here."

When he strode toward the trundiers, I crept after him. My pulse thundered in my ears. As we passed the smoldering coals in the firepit, I paused, grabbing a partly burned stick, wishing it was an AK-47.

As Garek approached Veskar, the beast shifted and snarled. He dipped his head and butted Garek with his snout while Garek stroked his nose and ruffled the creature's flat ears.

"What do you see?" Garek whispered and I almost expected the creature to answer.

I skittered up behind Garek.

"You did not remain at your tent," he said, not turning.

"I want to see what the sound is."

"You actually don't."

That stilled my heart. It thudded once. Twice. Then galloped, threatening to burst through my ribcage.

"What is it?" I asked, peering around but seeing nothing. The shriek hadn't been repeated.

"Duskhorde."

"What's a duskhorde?"

"Not what but who."

"Another alien race?"

He turned, and his face was revealed in the moonlight. A touch of humor flitted across his serious expression. "We are all aliens are we not? You and your friends as well."

"I guess. Who are the duskhorde?" And why weren't they mentioned in the literature?

Another shriek shook the night, this time so close I felt it ripple across my skin. Ferlaern males ran to their trundiers, taking flight.

Garek braced my arms, completely serious. "You need to go back to your tent and stay inside with Noah. Don't move or make a sound once you're inside no matter what you hear." He narrowed his gaze on the woods behind me. "We'll deal with this."

While I wanted to stand beside him and take on whatever this challenge, he knew what he was doing. I stood up to John, but I've only taken two self-defense courses since.

I turned to leave him.

Human calls were echoed by the deeper tones of the Ferlaern, telling me the others were awake and as worried as me. Someone had built up the fire again, and the flames leaped in the air like a dance of fiery demons.

Shivers rushed across my skin and while I had no sense of precognition, I knew my earlier thought that everything was about to change was about to come true. For the good or bad? I'd know by morning.

Assuming we made it until morning.

I'd only taken a few steps when I turned back to Garek. He stood at Veskar's flank, about to mount the beast. Would he wing through the sky and defeat all threats? I had a feeling he could.

Actually, I had a feeling there wasn't much this male couldn't do if he tried.

"Tell me what the duskhorde is," I said again.

His flinty gaze met mine. "As you said, they are another race living on Ferlaern."

"Maybe they come in peace?" Though the shrieks echoing in the woods like monsters hunting prey suggested otherwise.

"There is no peace with the duskhorde."

"Why not? Has anyone tried to work with them?"

"They will not agree to anything but taking Earth females for breeders."

"But… Earth could make an agreement with them, too."

"They are not ones you would seek a truce with."

"Maybe we just need to ask?"

"They eat us, Piper."

My knees went weak, and I staggered. "Eat you?"

He strode over to me and held my arms, studying my face as if he felt the need to memorize my features. "It's their way. They will never accept peace, and they consume the flesh of those they vanquish." When numerous thuds echoed from the forest, his face froze. He nodded his head to the central area. "Get Noah. Gather the others and go stand in the river."

"You said to go inside my tent."

"It's too late."

My skin prickled. There were deadly creatures in the river. "Why the water? Whatever attacked Missy is there. We should hide or stay close to the fire."

"They do not fear fire."

"We have weapons."

"Where are they?"

"In the boxes." Why hadn't we unpacked them first? They weren't guns—they told us not to bring them. But they didn't forbid crossbows. Pepper spray. Tasers. Knives.

"There isn't time to unpack them." He cocked one eyebrow but only kindness shone in his eyes. "Do you know how to use them?"

"We all trained."

"Can you hit a moving being when it rushes toward you with fangs bared and claws extended?"

I gulped but lifted my chin. "I'll try."

My odds of hitting anything were not good,

though. Only now did I realize this. If someone—something—attacked, it would take sharpshooters to eliminate the threat, not a bunch of women who visited the training course once a week before departure.

"Too many are coming even if you could hit each one as it emerged from the woods," he said. "Their way is to rush all at once, to disarm their prey with numbers and fear."

"We need a barricade. A tall fence." If we lived inside a fortress, we could eliminate this threat. Although, trundiers could fly. They could soar over a fence. Maybe the duskhorde could, too. We needed a dome, then. A—

"They can climb. A barricade won't keep them out."

"Then why the hell are we building in this valley?"

"Your people insisted on it."

"My people are wrong."

He dipped his head forward but didn't voice agreement. "They've never come this far north. We didn't expect them to find you."

And now they had. "We'll go to the river, then. Are they afraid of water?"

"They avoid it if possible. You'll be safer there than anywhere else." He lifted his hand in a signal, and a few of the males near the fire grunted and ran this way. "We wing, but some of us will remain behind for protection."

There were only nine Ferlaern warrior. Would that be enough?

I nodded, my teeth chattering with terror.

"There are worse things in Ferlaern than the river barbid," he said. "I hoped to keep you from discovering this for a very long time."

"We knew there would be danger." But never like this.

"When you enter the water, keep a stick in hand and smack the barbids if they come near. They will leave you alone after that."

I started toward my tent. I needed to get to Noah. But I turned back.

He watched me.

"Be safe," I said. Silly to worry about this warrior when we were the defenseless ones.

"For you, I will," he said in a growly voice.

Though his words held a promise, I didn't have time to question what he meant. I needed to get to my son. I bolted for my tent. Tripping over a rock, I lurched forward. My hair tightened around my neck like a noose, and my lungs heaved.

While wings flapped behind me as the warriors took flight, I wove around my friends and those who remained behind for protection.

"Get to the river," I shouted. "Quickly!"

While some of the women ran toward the water, a few of us rushed to our tents for our children.

The shrieks in the woods grew louder. Branches broke and the forest seemed to cringe as duskhorde feet thundered in our direction.

I hit my tent at a flat-out run and shoved the entrance flaps aside. My pulse dropped a notch when I found Noah sleeping. I slammed to my knees beside him, scrambling to find his sneakers and shoving them onto his feet, tying them as he stirred.

Garbled, guttural howls were punctuated by a high-pitched, quivering sound from the sky. Was the second the trundiers?

"Don't wanna get up," Noah mumbled, his arms flailing. "Wanna sleep, Mommy."

"It's okay, baby. You sleep. I just have to…take you somewhere." Earlier, it was all I could do to carry him, but with adrenalin surging through me, it was easy to scoop him up, wrapping him in his favorite blanket. With a sharp pivot, I rushed from the tent and joined the others hurrying toward the river at the urging of the remaining Ferlaern warriors. They had weapons out, and determination in their eyes.

A few kids cried while others went deathly silent as if they sensed they were being hunted and making a sound would draw the predators near.

The creepy Ferlaern who stared at me earlier stomped over to me. "Quick." He grabbed my arm and hauled me toward the water.

I nearly dropped Noah. "Slow down," I barked. "Please."

"They come," he said in a softer tone. "You have to hurry."

I broke into a run. My arms ached and my muscles spasmed as I held Noah close. Thankfully, he slept. I prayed he'd sleep through the upcoming attack.

The Ferlaern's fingers tightened on my arm. "If you wish…"

I shot him a questioning glance.

"I could take you somewhere where you and your fledgling would never need to fear."

"Garek is watching over us."

He sneered. "Garek can barely watch over himself."

"I'm staying here."

A growl rumbled in his chest, and his lips thinned, but I didn't have any interest in placating him.

"Get away from me. Go…do something useful."

The plates on his brow tightened but he backed away.

My attention was caught by something erupting from the woods. Pausing, the male—he wore no clothing, and he had a sizeable cock—looked around with his big, knobby head jutting from his hunched shoulders. Dark fur draped down his torso, and a single horn speared from his head. His beady red eyes locked onto me and the others running toward the river. With a shriek, he pivoted on his hooves and raced in our direction, leaping over our building materials like they were piles of kid's blocks.

I shuddered. A barricade would not stop these aliens.

One of the women screamed.

The Ferlaern at my side snarled. His weapon, a spiked mace I wouldn't be able to swing even if I could lift it, clunked on the ground. He lifted me and while I clung to Noah, he raced toward the water. Not stopping at the bank, he leaped, plunging down and landing where it was waist deep. He lowered me to my feet and raced back up the bank. He swept his weapon off the ground and bellowed as he ran toward the duskhorde streaming from the woods.

The Ferlaern were outnumbered, but their lack of numbers was more than a match for the attackers. Weapons swung through the air, connecting with heads, sending the hairy aliens tumbling across the ground. Some roared to their feet and attacked the Ferlaern while others remained where they fell, twitching.

"I'm scared," Noah mumbled against my chest. "Make the monsters go away, Mommy. Please!"

If only I could.

I clung to him, shielding his face as if me putting my fingers over his eyes could block him from seeing the fury raging above us on the open plain.

Something bumped my hip.

Shuddering and releasing jerky cries, I shifted Noah to my hip and speared my branch into the water. It hit something hard, and the river shark swam away. Around me, women cried out as other huge fish came near. They also used their sticks, driving off the river predators. Garek was right, if you showed them force, they left you alone. If only the duskhorde were as easily beaten back.

Three duskhorde left the pack, getting past the Ferlaern. They ran toward the river, their red eyes searing across my flesh with blood-curdling intent.

We backed up until we stood in chest-deep water,

huddling together like we could somehow protect each other with sticks. One woman shot a slingshot, hitting a duskhorde guy square in the forehead with a stone. He tumbled down the bank and lay still. But he was one of many, and others leaped forward to take his place.

More shots were fired but there were too many duskhorde and too few slingshot rocks.

A couple of the women sobbed. I remained stoic, determined not to panic in front of Noah. It was stupid, really. Like me being scared would make him feel better?

If I were alone, I'd run screaming, with terror bolting through me.

Wing flapped, and the trundiers spiraled down from the sky. They slammed into the beasts, sending them flying like candlepins. Dark blood spurted as Ferlaern swords sliced through necks and were buried deep in the other aliens' sides.

With the fliers, it appeared to be a rout. Yet my body shook. Horror and fear whipped around inside me, flaying me raw.

"Fuck," Rayne said, sidling close to me. She held her daughter, Missy, and the little girl clung to Rayne's neck; her legs wrapped around her mom's waist. The child's terrified gaze never left the water and whimpers erupted from her throat. Rayne tried to comfort her, but how could she? Big fish circled us, and death was roaring toward us like a freight train off the tracks above us.

Garek was right. There were worse things in Ferlaern than the barbids.

One of the duskhorde was hit by a warrior. He stumbled backward, into the fire. As he writhed and screamed, burning logs rolled out, toward our tents.

A whoof, and our tents ignited.

9

Garek

I wrenched my short sword from the spine of a dusklen. Another leaped through the air, intent on ripping apart my throat. With a guttural cry, I slashed out. My weapon cut deep, sinking past the male's fur-coated, armored body, impaling to the hilt.

The dusklen writhed, his claws scrambling on my mount, but they didn't penetrate Veskar's thick hide. In its death throes, the male slithered to the ground. I yanked my blade from his chest as he tumbled away.

Others raced toward the river. Fuck. The women. With a tap of my heels, Veskar took flight, snarling. He hated the duskhorde as much as I did. They weren't picky about who or what they ate and raids on trundier eggs and hatchlings used to be a common occurrence until we drove the duskhorde from our valleys.

I didn't fear they'd kill the females. They'd take them, and consent would no longer be a part of their future.

Veskar soared past the lead dusklen, ripping off the male's head as he passed. He spit it out and it bounced toward the woods. Spinning, my trundier flew over the writhing, headless dusklen and slammed into the others rushing toward the river.

My short sword flashed out, severing an arm. The male wrenched sideways and skidded across the ground. Undeterred, he rose to his feet and lumbered toward the river.

Veskar reeled and winged that way. As he swept over the male, I plunged my blade down through the male's spine. He collapsed forward, dead before he hit the ground.

Around me, my friends and clansmates finished off the horde eager to reach the females standing bravely in the river.

Shrieking, the ones in the back of the pack spun and ran into the forest. We flew after them but reeled upward before entering the woods. The duskhorde hunted forests at night. They'd wait and attack, picking us off one by one. We wouldn't be able to fight as one unit; we'd be split by vegetation. We could take care of the rest of them at dawn.

Distressed cries sent me spinning, and I reeled Veskar around, my chest tight.

The women splashed from the river, toward their tent village, but it was too late. Fire raged through the simple canvas structures, and most were completely engulfed.

I landed Veskar and slid down his side then ran to intercept the women.

They appeared unharmed, but my gaze sought Piper. Noah clung to her side, tears streaking through the soot on his face. When she saw me, she took her son's hand and ran around the fire and right up to me.

"You're not hurt?" she asked, her voice full of panic. Streaks lined her face, and I couldn't resist smudging them away with my thumbs.

"I'm fine," I said. She leaned into my touch and for one munette, her eyes closed. "You and Noah…?"

"They didn't come near us. Because of you guys, they didn't come near." Her voice broke. "I can't thank you enough." Her arms clumsily went around me in a hug before she stepped backward. "Oh. I'm sorry. Boundaries are usually my thing but—"

"I do not mind." I tugged her close and held her while she shivered.

Smoke boiled into the sky and hung around the low area like a funeral pyre, making everyone cough.

"In the river…" She trembled. "A barbid bumped me. Back home, we have creatures like this in the ocean. Sharks. You were right. I smacked it and it went away." Fresh tears sprang up in her eyes. She eased away from me and turned toward the smoldering tents. "What are we going to do? We don't have any other tents, and we can't sleep on the ground." Quakes took over her body, and she tucked her son close to her side. "We're going to d—" Her mouth snapped closed before she said it, and terror rang in her voice. "We can't sleep outside. They'll…" Her arm stroked down her youngling's back. "They'll come back. We can't sleep outside."

I tugged her back against my chest, my arms going around her while she held her son. They trembled, and I couldn't do anything to reassure them. The duskhorde encroached on our winter hunting grounds but they hadn't come this far inland for many cycles.

"I'm afraid," she said, turning to press her face against my skin. She spoke so low only I could hear. "If we build here, they'll kill us when we're gardening or foraging. In our beds when we're most vulnerable. I was going to go into the woods to set snares tomorrow!" Her voice dropped to almost nothing, and though I tightened my arms around her, this would be little comfort. "They'll never stop, will they?"

If only I could find a way to give her comfort.

"I don't know what to do, Garek," she whimpered. "How can I keep my boy…" Tears welled in her eyes all over again. "I left a nightmare on Earth only to find it all over again here."

This broke me. I hadn't been able to keep her from harm.

"You can live with us until we build your village," I offered softly by her ear.

"Build where? I don't want to come back here. They'll return." Anxiety lifted her voice. "They'll come back, and they'll hurt us!"

"I promise, you'll be safe." Though I wasn't sure where we'd build their homes. The base of our valley was coated with thick vegetation and our homes were in the forest. "For now, we have plenty of space in our domits."

Too many empty homes. We were haunted by the loss of our fledglings and females.

"All right. We'll go with you," she said with strength returning in her voice. She tugged Noah between us and laid her head against my chest. "We need to stay together so we can protect each other, though I'm not sure what good we'll do. You and your clansmen did the hard work."

Noah eased out from between us to lean against his mother's side, facing the smoldering tents. Wails rang out as the females threw buckets of water on what was left. Even the younglings stood mutely, watching their mothers.

"I vow right now that you will never want," I said. "Never have a need I will not fulfill."

I cupped her face and with the smoke swirling around us, I kissed her, tenderly at first but with growing need. Searing my promise with my flesh.

She met my lips with a need of her own, and it sparked a fire within me, one only she could extinguish. Our lips moved together and for this munette, I felt pure bliss. I never dreamed… Never hoped.

Her hands splayed across my arms, holding me tight before she eased back.

"Noah," she whispered. "I…" Stepping away, she touched her lips swollen from mine. Her mouth opened, but she swallowed her words, patting her youngling's shoulder.

Noah stared toward the ruined tents. The horror of this night would linger for a long time. We needed to leave this place and pray the duskhorde did not follow.

Piper's chest rattled. When she looked up at me, tears streaked down her face. "Take us away from here, please?"

10

Piper

I kissed him, and I wanted to do it again.

Traitorous body. It led me into danger. Needing Garek was playing with fire.

I was savvy enough to know this wasn't something instigated by sadness or my horror about what happened. We hadn't been caught up in the moment. From the first time I met him, I wanted him. No use denying that. The big question was: what would I do about it? We came here to meet males and promised to consider a serious relationship. Back on Earth, it was easy to believe I wanted nothing from any of them.

Until I met Garek.

Maybe there wasn't anything I had to do. *He* could've been overcome by the moment.

I'd watch him and see where this went next, if anywhere.

By the time dawn crested the sky, we'd sorted through what remained of our things and packed them in bags secured to the trundier's spines. There were too few bags. Other than random items of clothing and the boxes we hadn't unpacked yet, we had nothing but what we went to bed in—and that was still damp from plunging into the river.

I was grateful I found one of my smaller bags with two pairs of jeans and a few t-shirts for each of us in a duffel left outside our tent. We dressed and tucked away our nightclothes for later.

The tents hadn't been much. They were meant to be temporary until we built permanent structures. Now I didn't want to build. Not here, anyway, in the place where tragedy struck before we could begin to feel complacent.

We were homeless. Vulnerable. Solely dependent on the Ferlaern. This wasn't our intent when we came here. We were determined to bring what we needed to start a new life. We wanted independence.

My dream of a new wild west fell apart in a flash.

As we skittered around the campsite gathering things, we kept half our attention on the woods. Jumpy, I was poised to bolt at the first shriek, but the duskhorde didn't return. Not yet anyway.

As soon as the sun rose, Garek sent three warriors into the woods, and they returned about an hour after they left. When Garek approached them, they spoke softly together, shaking their heads.

I didn't want to ask, but I had to. I strode over to them. "Did you find them?" Did they drive them away forever? While living in this location was no longer an option, we could move to another part of the valley if we could feel confident the horde would not return.

"They didn't," Garek said.

"They fled, then?" That brightened my somber mood. "They won't return?"

The four males exchanged heavy glances then universally stared at their shifting feet.

"They'll return," Garek said in such a grim tone, it made my heart stop. "They always return."

"Why do you say that?" My voice filled with wild panic. "You chased them away. Killed a bunch of them. They learned their lesson."

Garek's clansmen looked from me to Garek before melting to the side and shuffling around us to join the others.

Garek stared toward the forest, his hand gliding along the handle of the short sword encased in the sheath on his chest. "There's no lesson they will ever learn. I wish I could tell you they're gone forever, but this isn't their way." He fully faced me. His fingers, so big and what should be clumsy, carefully stroked my face. "They saw you. All of you. And they're desperate for females."

"They would mate with us."

"A mating is not what they seek. They rut."

Shivers tracked through me, and my pulse pounded in my throat. "We'll face them. Defeat them." Even as I said it, I knew my words were foolish. What good had we been last night? The Ferlaern saved the day. "There's no way to build something they can't climb or leap onto?"

"Not here. I'm sorry."

I shrugged through my tears, hating that I couldn't stop them from pouring down my face. Why was I clinging to this place? It meant nothing more to me than the bunk I slept in on the ship we traveled to get here.

Home was where the heart is. That's what my mom always said. And that was Noah. He was safe—for now—and I would make sure that didn't change.

Garek would help; I trusted him to do that.

"We'll come back here for your building materials and transport them to the valley with our domits. I don't know how we'll use them, but we'll keep them safe until you decide. In between then, there are empty domits in our valley. Too many." His sigh bled from his lungs. "It's not your…feral west, but you're welcome to remain there as long as you need a home."

"Thank you." Our plan might still come true. It needed to change, adapt to Ferlaern, just like we had to.

"There is one thing I still need to do before we can leave," he said, his gaze locked beyond me on someone else. When I turned, I found the creepy alien watching us with a mix of irritation and anger on his segmented face.

"Who is he?"

"Skydar? Someone who's eager to crown himself king."

"You don't have kings here, do you?"

"No, but we crown warlords."

"How?"

"That remains to be seen and that's why I have to leave you for a brief time."

Vague, but I wouldn't press him. He had a task to do, and so did I. He wasn't obligated to me; he didn't have to hang around and keep me company.

Beyond Skydar and high up, what looked like a flock of huge birds winged this way. Trundiers.

"Is that the rest of your clansmen?" I asked, watching as they drew closer. They circled overhead.

"Some. Others stayed at the eyrie to ensure it was safe. These clansmen will remain here with you and the others while a few of us go into the mountains."

"You mentioned a ceremony last night."

"It's vital to my clan but it won't take long." He turned me to face him, his hands gripping my upper arms, though gently. "Will you feel secure here with them?"

A glance over my shoulder showed about twenty trundiers landing and an equal number of brawny alien males dismounting.

"You chased the duskhorde off with only nine Ferlaern. I'm sure this many watching over us will keep us from harm. Go." I nudged his side and flashed him the best smile I could drum up given the circumstances. "We'll be here when you return."

He stroked my face again. "There are many things I wish to say to you, but this is not the time."

And I wasn't sure I was ready for that time. Not yet. The fact that I added yet to my internal statement hit hard. Was I softening to him already? There was danger in that.

Somehow, I sensed Garek would not hurt me. Not me or Noah. But I had to be sure.

I stepped back so he could go. "I'll see you in a bit." Then I turned and strode over to the others still picking through the boxes we hadn't yet sorted.

Four trundiers took flight, and I shielded my face from the sun. As they flew toward the mountains, Garek's skin gleamed, a sharp contrast to Veskar's walnut color, like he was a precious jewel in a dark setting.

I watched them until they were specks in the sky.

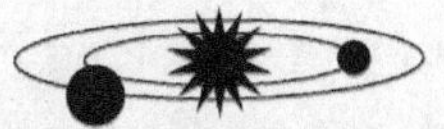

11

Garek

We landed our trundiers on the cliff. Skydar and his second jumped off their mounts, saying nothing. They pivoted and strode over to the cave entrance to wait. There was no need for conversation between us. We would test the powldron and pray it chose the right male. If it did not select either of us, it would be held until another from my clan wished to test it.

I slid off Veskar, landing on the ground beside Narcial, the senior spiritual leader of our clans.

"Thank you for coming," I said, holding her forearms. Her grayed hair sifted across her sturdy shoulders in the light breeze. We touched foreheads in greeting before stepping apart.

"I welcome participating in this event," Narcial said in a cheery voice. "An unmatched powldron is a rarity. It has been many cycles since I've overseen a new melding."

The last new melding took place over one hundred cycles ago, when a clan warlord drowned in the vast sea. His body and powldron were never recovered, and three of the males in his clan tested an available powldron. I didn't know how long it had been since a father decided not to pass his powldron to his eldest son. Shame flooded me all over again. I was proud I won leadership of our clan by my strength and wits, but it burned that I would not be granted full warlord status because of my father's actions.

If this powldron chose me, I would pass it to my own fledgling son or daughter. For some reason, Noah sprang to mind, though that made no sense. He was an Earthling, not a Ferlaern. He was not a part of our ways.

"You're ready?" Narcial asked. Her gaze left mine and narrowed on the two males shuffling their boots near the cave entrance. She turned back and rolled her eyes. The segmented golden skin on her forehead wrinkled.

I chuckled, though it came out more nervous than I liked.

Skydar released a disgusted grunt. "Why do we linger here when we have a powldron to bestow?" His tail whipped back and forth behind him. Leave it to him to ignore the proper protocols. He had one goal in mind, and it was not leading. He wished to rule, to make demands he knew our clan would have no wish to fulfill.

I wasn't sure what I'd do if the powldron melded with him instead of me. No longer a leader, I could join another clan, or I could remain with ours and serve as a hunter or builder—one of my true skills. I enjoyed constructing something new, which was why I was excited when I saw the Earthling's plans for their homes. While I couldn't see how they'd hold up to the threats on my planet, they were unlike anything on Ferlaern.

Narcial leaned close to me, her graying black hair sweeping across her shoulders. The pale lavender strands gleamed in the sunlight. "Do ensure you are chosen, son," she said dryly, her attention cutting to Skydar. "I cannot stomach following his lead."

"I'll do my best, elder," I said, giving her a short bow.

"Durran." Narcial nodded to my friend standing nearby. He'd serve as my second, just as Abskin stood with Skydar. In sunslices long ago, when a clan was left without a warlord, a battle was fought, and the two best warriors would test the powldron. That part of the ceremony fell away in the past. Now two individuals—male or female—were selected by the clan. Skydar had a solid following, as did I.

"Good luck, friend," Durran said, bracing my arms and lightly connecting our foreheads.

"Thank you."

"No matter what happens, you are worthy."

Only my scarred friend would see my bravado to the uneasy youngling still lurking inside.

"You were young, but we would've followed you," he said. "Never doubt that."

"My father did not agree."

"Then *he* is the one who is unworthy—of you."

Closing my eyes, I nodded as his words sunk through me. My heart lightened, and I felt more prepared to face my fate. My fingers tightened on his arms, and I touched foreheads again, unsure where I would be without the support of my friends.

We moved around our trundiers, and my attention fell on the chest Narcial had dropped beside the cave entrance. She arrived last evening to prepare for the ceremony.

The chest and powldron came from the Driegons. Descended from dragons, the Driegon race lived in caverns below the surface on a planet a few sunslice's space travel from here. They discovered the chest in a previously unknown level of their ruling castle and their elder knew right away the purpose of the powldron. Who knows how it ended up on a different planet? She reached out to us, and we arranged to collect it.

"We are ready?" I asked the others.

Skydar snorted again, but Durran and Abskin each lifted one side of the trunk. The powldron inside shifted, scraping as it slid across the bottom.

We strode through the wide entrance of the cave, following Narcial. For many generations and before the duskhorde invaded and our clans moved to the valleys to settle in domits, we held ceremonies here. The first markings of a youngling. The remembrance of an aged one who died. The lifting of warlords. Since we had to be in this area to greet the Earthlings, it made sense to use a traditional cave for the testing ceremony.

Leaving the narrow tunnel, we emerged into a decent-sized cave alive with light. The fire Narcial lit blazed in the pit built in the center of the chamber. Soot coated the rock circle and the smooth dirt beyond. The flames reflected on us many times over from the clear crystal covering the inner walls and ceiling of the cave. Huge spires jutted down from the ceiling and thrust up from the floor around the ceremonial circle.

Durran and Abskin lowered the chest on the ground within the circle then backed away to the far-right wall. They were here to observe and serve as heralds should the powldron choose Skydar or me.

Narcial gestured for me to stand on one side of the circle and Skydar the other. We faced each other with grim expressions, making a triangle outside the fire with the chest the third point.

My heart thudded a rapid beat in my chest. When asked yesterday if I was nervous, it was easy to scoff with my friends. Now I faced my defining munette. I would leave this cave a warlord or be demoted to a simple clansman.

I did not wish to fail today but my future belonged to the fates.

Narcial remained outside the circle. She lifted her hands, her eyes closed as she sang something in ancient Ferlaern. The soft mutterings soothed my soul, and I sunk into a relaxed feeling, my gaze locked on the fire.

"You think this is yours already," Skydar said in a low voice, wrenching me from my trance. "The female, as well. But you know nothing. She will be mine, as will the powldron."

I lifted one brow ridge and did not point out that Piper returned my kiss. She sought shelter in my arms, not his.

"Enough, Skydar," Narcial growled, barely breaking her chant to send the rebuke. "Silence."

Again, I wondered how fate had led me here. How I went from a fledgling trusting his role in life to an adult struggling to hold onto power that in every other clan was gifted.

Some things are worth fighting for, however. I was proud of how I held onto my leadership with my body and mind. I earned my right to be here.

And Piper? She was definitely worth fighting for. Once this was settled—no matter how it was settled— I would ask to court her. Would she agree to be my mate?

Narcial strode to the chest and stooped down in front of it. She lifted her hands over it and hummed, but she didn't touch the scarred wooden surface. Rising, she walked around the circle in one direction then the other before stopping in front of the chest again. She stooped down on her knees and lifted her hands over the chest, mumbling more ancient Ferlaern.

I ached to view the powldron. Would I recognize it as mine before touching it?

Why had my father chosen to take our family

powldron to the grave with him? It not only burned, but it also hurt. I thought we were close, that he trusted me. Instead, he cast my future aside as if I were nothing.

Narcial went silent. The world ticked around us, the silence broken only by the shuffle of feet and the crackle of the fire. We watched. Waited. Bending forward, Narcial blew on the fastener mounted in the front of the chest. A click echoed in the cave, and the lid creaked open.

I wanted to stride over to the chest and claim the powldron, to prove to the world, if not myself, that I was the one fated to wear it, but protocols must be followed.

"Who will choose first?" Narcial asked.

"Me," Skydar said, stepping forward.

Narcial merely stared at him, and Skydar paused. He stepped backward, into the spot Narcial initially placed him, his fuming gaze shooting across the fire to meet mine. "I wish to go first."

"The powldron chooses outside of turns," Narcial said. Her attention shifted to me. "What say you, Garek?"

"Let him go first. Then it's truly fate if the powldron waits to choose me, wouldn't you say?"

Narcial grunted. "This is true, and your answer is the reply of a leader."

I held my smile at the dig directed at Skydar who hadn't won a battle that would allow him to claim leadership of our clan if we followed the old ways.

This hadn't stopped him from giving direction whenever he felt no one would protest.

It was difficult enough managing a clan of hundreds of warriors, plus a few children and females, let alone deal with hints of insurrection. Skydar didn't like the old ways yet here he was, awaiting a chance to be chosen by a powldron.

"Come forward, youngling," Narcial said with a wave to Skydar. "From what I heard from the Driegon elder, this powldron is one unlike any I have seen before. I am curious to discover who it will choose."

"What do I do?" Skydar asked in a voice that only now betrayed his unease with the entire process. He stopped beside the chest and stared down with intense longing.

"You reach in and take the powldron."

"That's it?" Skydar's triumphant gaze shot to me. "It's simple."

"Taking is not claiming and the powldron will still decide," Narcial said, stepping back three paces to stop on the outer rim of the circle. "Take the powldron and wear it. If it chooses you, it will meld."

"Does it…" Skydar swallowed deeply, and his eyes met his second's before shooting back to the elder. "Does it hurt?"

"I have not been chosen," Narcial said. "So, I cannot truly say. Perhaps you'll soon be able to tell us."

"Yes," Skydar hissed. "I'll do it." His hands twitched at his sides, and his tail whipped back and forth, sending air shooting at the fire. The coals grabbed hold of it and blazed brighter. The flames shifted in a heady dance, their rich colors reflecting off the crystals.

He stepped around to the front of the chest and stooped down to its level. His horns jutted forward, and his tusks gleamed in the firelight. Leaning forward, he peered into the chest. "It is beautiful," he said in awe. "I never imagined. And it will be mine."

Do not be so certain, I thought, though I didn't voice the words. This was Skydar's time to shine if the fates deemed him worthy.

He reached into the chest and pulled out the powldron. About a forearm's length and flat, it gleamed in the light.

Durran gasped. I held mine back, though it was not easy. It *was* beautiful. Made up of deep blues and browns richer than the heartiest soil, plus silver steel, it appeared as untouched as when it was crafted from a living ednest tree then merged to the metal with fire. The ednest tree truly lived, an entity that could communicate with the world around it. It's said the trees grow in perfusion within the forests of undar, though no one has sought them for many generations. They guard their wood well, and only a master smythe can lull one long enough to take what he or she needs to craft a powldron.

Our last master smythe died many cycles ago. The secret for how they were created was lost with him as was his apprentice, one of our beloved females who died from the disease.

Knowing there would be no other powldron when my father chose not to pass his only made this one sweeter. It was a chance I never thought would come my way.

"Look at it and watch as it chooses," Skydar said. He pivoted around in a victory dance, the powldron held overhead before he stopped, facing my direction. "Watch me, Garek. You've had your turn with leadership. Now it and everything else I want is mine." He lowered the powldron onto his shoulder and from where I stood, it appeared to meld with his armored skin.

No.

It was a knife in the gut.

I was so sure it would wait for me. Was I wrong not to insist on going first? It was my right as our hard-fought leader to claim that role. But a powldron made its own choice and it appeared to have selected Skydar.

"Yes." He thrust both hands overhead and bellowed toward the ceiling. "It is mine!" His hands slapped down to his sides, and he rounded the chest, striding toward me. "There are many things I plan to do with our clan, but first, I will claim one certain female. It is only right that a warlord mate with the leader of the Earthling settlers." He stomped toward me, but when he started to lift his hands to touch me, he paused. His gaze shot to his shoulder and the powldron lying across it.

It dropped from his skin and hit the ground with a clatter.

"No." Skydar's guttural cry echoed in the cave. "It's mine." He reached toward it—

"Stop," Narcial said, her soft tone threaded through with granite. When she spoke, everyone listened, even a would-be warlord like Skylar.

Skylar froze with his hand hovering over the powldron.

"It did not choose you," Narcial said. She walked over and wedged herself between the powldron and Skydar. "You must back away and give the other contender equal chance."

"It melded with me," Skydar yelled. "I know it did. It is mine. I'm a warlord, prepared to assume command of our clan."

"You are a clansman," Narcial said gently.

She laid a reassuring hand on his arm, but he wrenched away. He backed up; his gaze wild.

"It will not choose you," he slurred to me. "I will have a second chance once you are finished." Growling and snapping his tusks, he stomped around the fire and retook his spot. His level gaze met mine. "Go ahead. Show the world you are nothing more than a pretend leader. Show us why your father did not pass his powldron to you."

Mere bluster on his part. This was not a trundier one tamed over a cycle, one that could choose to reject the warrior in favor for another at any given time. A powldron formed a symbiotic relationship with its wearer. While the male removed it at night to rest, it was a part of him always, functioning only for him until he passed it to another. It enhanced his skill in battle. It lent strength when the warlord was weak. And it was said to provide guidance in times of need.

"Garek?" Narcial said. "I don't want to lift it. Only one seeking to be warlord should touch it, and that's not me. I'm content in my role as our elder."

I nodded, my gaze never leaving the powldron. It gleamed in the firelight, and I swore it spoke only to me.

Come.

I bent down and studied it, not quite daring to touch it. This was the munette I've waited for most of my life. My sole chance. Once I tried, I would get no second chance. I could continue to serve as leader and fight for that right each cycle, but if one of the other clan's warlords decided to bring our clan beneath his wing, his say would outweigh mine. A leader was one step below a warlord, and if my leadership were not secured with a melded powldron, it could end at any time.

"You are afraid?" Skydar taunted. Abskin stepped forward and laid a restraining hand on his friend. Skydar shrugged him off, his greedy gaze training on the powldron. "Leave it. I will collect it on my way out."

A snap of my hand, and I grasped the powldron. Warmth glided across my fingers. Its smooth texture felt amazing. I swore the wood spoke to me but that was wishful thinking. I wanted this so much, not just for me but for our clan.

I am worthy, father. Truly. If only you had seen.

I straightened, holding the powldron out in front of me. The rich blue wood glistened in the firelight and beams arced off the metal.

Then I lifted it and laid it across my shoulder.

It bit deep, sinking its metal-spiked wooden fingers into my flesh.

"Ah," Narcial breathed, her eyes wide.

As it fused with me, I tipped my head back and roared.

12

Piper

While Garek and his friends were gone, we inventoried the things untouched by the fire and the duskhorde's rampage. Fortunately, our building materials were spared. As we sadly went through what was left, a Ferlaern warrior hovered near each of us, behaving like our own personal bodyguard. Two kept the children busy but nearby while we worked. They were unfailingly gracious to us as if we were precious china that if dropped, would shatter into a billion pieces.

We were just finishing up when the four Ferlaern winged overhead and dropped down to the ground.

Beasts that frightened me yesterday felt like tame pets when compared to the duskhorde. Funny how one night and an attack could change someone's perspective. The males dismounted and tension swirled through the air. What happened during the ceremony?

One of the males stepped forward and cleared his

throat. He flashed his tusks, and I couldn't help noting his gaze never left Rayne, though she was busy with Missy. "I present to you a warlord," he said in a gruff voice.

Grunts and stomping feet erupted from the males around us as Garek strode closer, moving to the head of the others.

Skydar's face twisted into a scowl but the expression wasn't much different than what he projected most of the time. The blinding white anger burning in his eyes was new, however. I recognized it like a doe did the sound of a shot in the woods. Only the strength of my will and steely determination kept me rooted when his heavy gaze locked onto me.

Meriwee stood beside me. We just finished sorting through a box of household supplies, setting aside things she suggested we might need in our new domits.

"Ah, Skydar," she said with a hollow sigh. When her gaze met mine, her eyes shimmered. "I hoped my brother would be chosen."

"Chosen by what?" I asked.

She shook her head and again, I admired how gorgeous her hair was, a rich black shot through with pale purple. Her horns—about four inches long—jutted from her forehead. "I'm sorry, but do you mind if I don't finish here? I want to go to my brother. He needs me."

"No, it's okay. I understand." Not really, but I was sure I'd learn what happened soon.

She rushed over to Skydar and spoke to him. His

lips tightened and his tail whipped behind him, but he said nothing, just glared at Garek and then me.

Garek walked right up to me and stopped, putting himself between us like he did last night. While I wanted to fight my own battles, I wasn't going to complain about the wall between me and Skydar.

He dipped his head forward as if prepared to introduce himself to me all over again. "It's finished," he said.

"That looks new," I said, jerking my chin toward a blue and silver swath of armor lying across his shoulder and partway down his arm. No straps held it in place; it appeared welded to his skin.

"My powldron," he said. The proud lift in his voice made me smile. He sounded so happy.

"A powldron sounds like something a gladiator would wear." Garek was as brawny, powerful, and commanding as any gladiator I ever imagined.

He frowned. "What is this glad…?"

"Long ago on Earth, gladiators fought to the death in a ring for the entertainment of those watching. Gladiators were lauded as the heroes of that time."

"We have nothing like this gladiator ring or battle here, though it is common for Ferlaern to fight for leadership of a clan."

"Is that what you did? I thought you were already the leader of your clan."

"I fought for leadership every cycle until now."

"Why only until now?"

His fingers traced along the powldron and he

flashed his tusks again. "This elevates me to a full warlord. A warlord is a lifetime appointment."

I could tell he was very proud of this honor.

"And that's what the ceremony was about? Bestowing warlord status to you?"

"Yes." He flicked a glance over his shoulder at Skydar. "The powldron chose me."

And not Skydar. No wonder he looked upset. Meriwee held his arm and continued to speak to him, but he appeared oblivious to her, glaring at us.

Nothing good was going to come from that guy. It didn't take my history with my ex to know that.

"Congratulations," I said.

He bowed, and his voice lifted. "I will work hard to live up to the standards of a warlord. This is something I have wanted for my entire adult life."

"The powldron?"

"Yes, and to be my clan's warlord. A leader fights each cycle to remain in charge but when someone is chosen by a powldron, he becomes a warlord and remains the clan's leader until he or she chooses to pass the powldron to a family member or someone else who is worthy."

"Are you your clan's first warlord?"

Clouds skated across his face and his gaze went solemn. "No. My father was warlord before me, but he did not give me his powldron."

Oh. "Why not?" Nosy of me, but I could tell how much this meant to him. I had a feeling Garek was hurt when his father didn't pass him the powldron.

"He…" His voice cracked. "I don't know. He just didn't."

"I'm sorry. I can tell this means a lot to you. Congratulations. He didn't give his to you, but you've found your own. I'd say that's fate."

His face cleared. "You're right. Fate has chosen. For cycles, I've dreamed of all the things I could do as full warlord."

"And now those dreams can start coming true." I was happy for him. He was a fearless yet kind leader. I imagined he was relieved he no longer had to battle to maintain his leadership in the clan.

More stomps and grunts behind me sent me spinning to find most of the Ferlaern had gathered close.

"We have much to do," Garek said to all of us. "Is everything ready?"

One of the warriors stepped up beside me. He placed his closed fist on his shoulder. "We're prepared to depart when you are, warlord."

Garek's gaze sought mine. "The sooner we leave, the better." Squinting, his eyes swept the forest. We heard nothing unusual while we worked either because the duskhorde left or they didn't dare challenge so many warriors. But I didn't want to be here come nightfall. "Do you have everything you need?" he asked me.

"Let me grab the last few things I was sorting through to add with the others." I nodded to the bags waiting near the resting trundier. "We don't have much left." My voice broke for the fifty-billionth time and my eyes stung with tears. I still couldn't believe what happened, what I lost. I hadn't brought many personal items from Earth, just photo albums and a few keepsakes from my mom, but they were gone. Only half-charred bits remained. I sorted through them and found one baby picture of Noah with a scorched edge. It gutted me to lose so many keepsakes.

"You and Noah will ride with me," Garek said. "If this is acceptable."

Skydar growled, and his heavy gaze pinned me in place. "She could also ride with me."

I shuffled my feet. Really. Skydar? "Oh, I..."

"She will ride with me," Garek said pleasantly, though his voice held a hint of steel. His and Skydar's gazes dueled but the other males' dropped, I assumed because of Garek's new warlord status.

Did Skydar think I would shrug aside Garek and agree to ride with him? I gave him no indication I was interested. The thought of getting close to him made my skin crawl. Perhaps he thought his invitation to "take off" with him last night was his version of asking me out on a date. I needed to learn the Ferlaern cues before I agreed to something I shouldn't and make a big mistake.

"Thank you for the offer," I said to Garek. "Noah and I would be happy to ride with you." I turned, my attention landing on my son playing with the other children under the watchful gaze of two Ferlaern warriors. I lifted my voice. "Noah? It's time to go, honey."

My son raced over. He hugged my side and tipped

his face back to look up at me. "Where are we going, Mom? Isn't this our settlement?"

"It was but for now, we're going to live with Garek."

"Really?" Noah breathed, turning his adoring gaze Garek's way. "Really live with him, like we're a family?"

"Oh, no," I hurried to say, my face overheating. I shot Garek a look full of apology. "We're not going to truly live with—"

"You will stay in my domit," Garek said. "If that is also acceptable."

"What exactly does that mean, stay in your domit?"

And why did my skin tingle at the thought? Nothing had changed. I was still me, a woman determined to maintain her autonomy, someone who wasn't sure she wanted to try again with another male. I was warming to Garek, but we were just friends.

Friends who kissed.

Okay, so maybe friends with limited benefits, but those benefits didn't extend very far.

"It means you'll stay in my domit," he explained. "I'll find…another for the time being."

I squirmed. He'd give up his home for us? "We can't take your domit."

"Of course, you can."

"But where will you sleep?"

He shrugged and the new armor moved with him as seamlessly as if it was part of his arm. "There are bed furs in the warrior's training quarters. And other domits I can make habitable."

"Then we'll take one of those."

"Please," he said. "I'd feel better if you were in my domit. It's comfortable where the others will need cleaning and set up before they are ready for you and Noah."

"Okay," I said. "I guess that could work, but only for a short time. You need to have your home, and we need to create our own."

"Your home is wherever you choose, maidling," he said gruffly.

What did maidling mean? It sounded like an endearment, but it couldn't be.

"I assume we'll build our homes once you've… routed the duskhorde?" Was that the right term, routed? We couldn't build in a place they might attack.

"Once we're home, we can discuss what we'll do moving forward. And once things feel normal again, I would like—"

Missy ran up, giggling, with a female Ferlaern warrior chasing her. She darted between me and Garek, cutting off whatever he planned to say.

I was curious but would ask him about it later.

The female warrior growled and huffed, and Missy's peals of laughter filled the air as she raced around the others, hiding behind her mom to peek.

The kids were solemn this morning but as the day warmed, so did they, until they ran around like nothing happened. Only the adults appeared to still bear the scars of last night. Plus, Savvy, Josie's thirteen-year-old daughter. Shadows haunted her eyes and she cringed whenever a crack sounded from the woods.

She came forward, holding Alexa's twins' hands. Alexa followed, carrying bags.

Garek stepped back and directed the other warriors, matching some with each of the women. As the twins couldn't both ride with Alexa, Savvy offered to take one on her lap with whoever she rode with.

I lifted my last bag onto my shoulder, and we trudged away from our smoldering tent village to the trundiers who shifted and rose to their feet.

While my friends were guided by the other warriors, Garek led me and Noah to Veskar. Last night, this beast ripped heads off the duskhorde. The old me would tremble at the idea of getting close to a beast capable of such a horrifying act. Instead, I wanted to kiss his snout.

But riding…?

"I'm a little afraid of heights," I said softly.

"Mom," Noah said. "It's gonna be okay. Just pretend you're at the top of the slide at the park. That was fun, right?" He tilted his head, watching me.

I gave him a wan smile. "Sure. Top of the slide. No problem." I hadn't enjoyed sitting at the top of the slide, either, but other moms were watching, so I hadn't squealed in fright.

My hand shook, and my knees weren't doing any better. Maybe I could close my eyes and imagine I was on a merry-go-round.

As we approached, Veskar's spiked tail whipped

back and forth, and he huffed. As he vaguely resembled a cross between a hornet and a dragon, I almost expected fire to blast from his snout.

Noah left me and raced right up to him, and my pulse jumped. I scurried closer and placed my hands on my son's shoulders, prepared to wrench him back if Veskar turned vicious, but the beast's head dropped, and he nudged Noah like a horse might a friendly child holding out an apple.

Garek reached out and Veskar snorted against his palm. The beast's curious gaze turned to me as if I were the only one who hadn't introduced themselves.

I wasn't afraid to touch him. Well, not completely. But jeez, he was as big as one of those fancy campers, the kind that had a full bedroom, a kitchen, and a bathroom.

But this was my new life. Not that I thought I'd tame my own trundier, but I had a feeling it wouldn't be long before Noah begged to do so. What would I say? I wanted to wrap cotton around him to keep him safe, but our children were the bridge between Earth and the Ferlaern. If we—meaning our future generations—were going to get along, we all had to give. Earthlings were the strangers here, the true aliens. It was natural we'd give the most.

I held out my hand, pretending this was a giant horse. It sure wasn't easy.

Veskar delicately sniffed it. Then he took a step forward and nudged my belly in play. I tried to push out a laugh, but my body shook, and my pulse floundered in my throat.

"See?" Garek said. "He likes you."

I snorted. "Maybe." At least he wasn't biting my head off.

"I'm gonna ride him?" Noah exclaimed. "Really, really ride him?"

I rubbed his shoulder. "All the way to the Ferlaern's eyrie."

"Awesome," he breathed. He scooted around to Veskar's side and stood staring up at the huge beast. "How do I climb him? Do I just like, do it?"

"I'll help you mount," Garek said. After giving me a grin, he strode to Noah and stooped down in front of my son. "Veskar told me he cannot wait to give you a ride."

Noah's gaze flitted to mine, seeking permission, and a soft light bloomed in his eyes.

Garek was good for my son.

Good for me, too.

"I'm taking you and your mother to the valley we call home," Garek said. "You'll be safe there."

Would we? That remained to be seen.

My gaze swept the open area I'd already begun to think of as home, and my heart pinched.

I felt raw, like I suffered a lethal hit and the wound kept seeping. I wasn't sure I'd ever feel normal—feel hope—again. I thought I found it when I left earth only to see it trampled beneath the feet of the duskhorde.

"I'm excited," I said bravely, eagerly, as I skirted around Veskar's head to join them. Actually I was a tad nervous. Who wouldn't be? I was about to climb onto the back of a giant hornet who would soar through the sky. "We'll both ride with Garek."

"One must use great care when mounting a brave trundier," Garek said with a twinkle in his sage eyes. "I'll show you?" Garek held his hand out to Noah, leaving the decision to him.

Without hesitating, Noah placed his tiny hand in Garek's huge one. Garek's fingers carefully curled, and he tugged Noah close.

"I will lift you up onto Veskar," he said. "There is a place for you on the front of his spine, and see this horn?" He nudged his head to the solitary spike where Veskar's neck met his back. "That is for you to hold onto."

Others had already looped the ties of their bags over the spike on the other trundiers.

"I won't fall, will I?" Noah asked in a shaky voice, his bravado gone.

"I won't let you," Garek vowed. His nod was for me, saying I could trust him.

Trust hadn't come easy for me after John but somehow, in a tiny place of my heart, I was convinced this male was worthy. He wouldn't hurt me or Noah. He wouldn't let us down.

Garek lifted Noah onto his own shoulder and stepped up onto the beast's haunch. From there, he placed Noah on the trundier who remained patiently resting on the ground like a cow chewing its cud.

From his perch on top, Noah's wide gaze met mine, and a mix of fear and excitement flashed across his face. "Mom." The word jerked out of him as he clung to the spike. "It's like…a little scary but also awesome. I can see everything from up here."

"You're next," Garek said, holding out his hand. He remained on the beast's haunch, leaving the decision to approach or back away to me.

"She should ride with me," Skydar said, coming up behind us. His hand glided along the back of my waist. "There's no need for you to carry two. Take the fledgling and I will keep her secure."

Garek grunted. "Piper has already agreed to ride with me. Both of them will."

"But I'm alone on my mount," Skydar said with a hint of derision in his voice. "There is no need for you to take triple on yours."

Garek grunted and lifted his hand. "Piper?"

"I want my son with me," I said, hoping to diffuse the tension. I stepped forward, away from Skydar's hand. Ever since last night, this guy made me uncomfortable. I'd long since learned to trust my instincts about men. Was it only last night? It felt like a week ago, back when our future appeared rosy. Now it was as dark as the scorched remains of our unformed village. "My son is scared, tired. He needs his mom."

The segmented plates on Skydar's face tightened.

I turned my back on him, facing Garek. "Thank you for offering to help. I'm not quite sure how to climb him."

Skydar grumbled and strode toward his mount.

Garek's face loosened, cuing me in on the fact that he wasn't as calm as he appeared. He dipped his head forward.

As trusting as Noah, I laid my hand in his.

A tingle traveled across his rough palm. It hitched up my arm, and I tugged free, staring down at it. I turned it over, expecting to find… I didn't know what, but it looked like it always had.

Garek's breath caught, and his intent gaze lifted to me. Watched me as if he expected me to say something profound. His hand went to his chest and his fingers splayed wide.

"Ferlaerns have two hearts," he said. He didn't sound very happy about it, though.

"Really?" I cocked my head. "I haven't heard that before." Wouldn't they have mentioned it in the literature?

"The second rarely awakens."

I frowned. "What does that mean—awakens?"

He shook his head, scattering his deep black hair and I swore the purple streaks brightened. "I will explain later. Come. The others are getting ready to depart. We have a long distance to travel before we reach my valley." He held out his hand again.

When we touched this time, it felt normal. Just pure, warm male meeting a female who was starting to dream about one particular alien. He pulled me close, and his woodsy scent hit me all over again. Heat flooded my body, and I wanted to press myself against him. Tip my head back. Kiss him.

So silly. Around us, the others mounted their beasts and loaded their bags on the creatures' spikes. They wouldn't wait for me to do whatever it was I ached to do with Garek before they took off.

"What happened when we touched?" I asked in a low voice. And what did the shock have to do with him having two hearts? "Was it static electricity?"

He shrugged. "Must be."

His gaze never left mine. His fingers rose and he hesitated before running the back of them down my cheek.

"We're going to ride?" I said, my belly fluttering. Awareness sunk into me for the first time in forever and while I had no idea where my son and I would find a home in the future, one thing was clear.

I wanted Garek.

13

Garek

Piper was my maelstrom mate.

A maelstrom was forbidden for a warlord. Warlords mated to create young, they did not allow a true matebond to form.

It snuck up on me when I least expected it. We touched earlier and I assumed a maelstrom wasn't possible with Piper. I was relieved because then I wouldn't be expected to choose between her and my clan.

If my soul did not recognize hers already, the thrum of my newly awakened, second heart would convince me.

How was this possible? There had been no maelstrom pairings for generations. Our second hearts remained silent.

Now that I was melded with a powldron, I needed to use this opportunity to solidify my unsettled clan. The duskhorde needed to be taught never to venture into our territory again. And we needed to decide what we would do with these humans.

"Garek?" Piper asked, her gaze taking in the others nearly ready to leave.

There were clear consequences for a warlord who formed a maelstrom bond with any female. I needed to decide what I would do.

"I need to lift you up onto Viskar," I said gruffly as if she did not already know this. If I put distance between her and me, would the mating urge fade and my second heart stop beating?

Awareness of her rushed across my skin like wildfire.

The moment we reached the eyrie, I would get her settled then walk away. Forget her even though my hearts shattered at the thought. If I did not make the choice, it would be made for me.

When my hands went around her waist, my cock twitched. The culier strands lining the surface elongated and vibrated.

Fuck.

Despite my mind's wish to resist her, my body had already succumbed. What was I going to do?

I lifted her and tucked her behind Noah, and her arms went around her son. Seeing her so gentle with her youngling softened me. It always would. She was a good mother, kind and tender with her child. Any male would be happy to mate with her.

I could barely suppress my growl at the thought of her choosing someone else.

If I could not claim her, I should let her go. Hell, I

should let Skydar carry her to our eyrie. She might awaken his second heart, and I could pretend mine didn't thrum in my chest only for her.

Later. I would encourage others to court her later.

Panic bloomed in her eyes as she settled herself on Veskar. "This is…interesting. It's so, um, high up."

I frowned. "High?"

"It's awesome," Noah breathed. Fearless, he leaned forward to stroke Veskar's neck. "I want a trundier. Can I have one, too?" He tipped his head back to plead with his mother. "He's like a big giant puppy."

"Not exactly, Noah," she said, her sparkling eyes meeting mine. "And let's wait and see about that. Our first goal is to build a home, not adopt…trundiers."

"If I had a trundier, I could name him and feed him and play with him. I could ride him everywhere. And once I have a sword like Garek, I could fight the monsters." Noah leaned back against Piper. "They won't scare you any longer, Mom."

"You're not getting a sword," she said firmly. "And you sure as hell are not fighting monsters." Her pleading gaze met mine. "Right, Garek?"

"Our fledglings start training when they are five, but they do not take on the horde for many cycles after that. Not until we are confident they are ready."

"That isn't reassuring, Garek."

"See, Mom?" Noah said, sharing a conspirator's smile with me. "I'm already behind. Three years! Will you train me, Garek, once I have my own trundier?"

"I'm not a weapons master but we have many in

our clan's eyrie. I'm sure one could fit you with a blunted weapon for practice."

"Awesome!" Noah leaned forward to stroke Veskar's neck again.

I leaped up behind Piper and settled my hips on Veskar's spine. This brought me close to Piper. I closed my eyes and willed my cock to behave.

"You mentioned the eyrie earlier," Piper said with a glance over her shoulder.

Due to the shape of Veskar's spine, there was no way I could avoid touching her, nestling against her body. I told myself I eased forward because I needed to hold onto her. I must keep her from falling.

There was no fooling myself, I wanted to be close to her.

My hearts craved her.

"I need to hold you while you support Noah," I said.

She practically sat on my lap.

Fuck.

"That's fine," she said. Did I hear tension in her voice? She rode a trundier for the first time. That was why.

"Once I have a practice sword, when do I get a trundier?" Noah asked as Piper's arms secured around him. "Will it be a big one like Veskar or can I raise one from a baby?"

"After the trundiers hatch, we slowly tame them," I said.

"This is even better than a puppy," Noah said in awe. "Please Mom? Can I tame a trundier, too?"

"You're filling my son with dreams that can't come true," she said softly.

I grunted. "Why not?"

"Because he's human, not Ferlaern."

"To be Ferlaern, one merely needs to join a clan."

"Awesome!" Noah said. "Can I join your clan, Garek?"

"We'll see, youngling. There is much that must be done before something like that can happen."

His small shoulders curled forward. "Aw, I want it to happen now."

"First, we must travel." Which meant sitting close to Piper for many sunslices. Why had I not thought this through? Yet offering her a place with Skydar was not an option. My maelstrom mate would ride with me.

"Okay," Noah said. "It's still going to be awesome to ride on Veskar."

My face cracked with my smile, making me realize how long it had been since I flashed my feelings.

"Hold on, honey," she said, her arms tightening around him. "We're going to fly way up high, so no horsing around."

"What is this horsing?" I asked as others took wing around us.

"Playing when he should be serious while riding."

"Staring down at the drop will settle him," I said.

With a nudge of my legs, I told Veskar what I wished. He leaped from the ground and his wings flicked out. We soared up into the sky, winging behind the others.

"Oh, shit," she said. She kept one hand around her son's waist, and the other landed on my thigh, gripping the fabric of my pants. "I don't…"

"Are you alright?" I asked.

"Mom's afraid of heights," Noah explained. "When we rode on the tilt-a-whirl at the fair, she puked."

"I'm not going to puke, Noah," she said, her fingers blanching where they clutched my pants.

"Would it help if I held onto you?" I asked, almost hating to say it. I wanted to hold her. Always. But that would meld our bodies together.

I needed to stop thinking about her body pressed against mine.

"Ahhh," Piper squealed, leaning back in my arms. "Oh, shit. Hell. Fuck."

"Mom," Noah exclaimed. "That's a lotta swearing. You're gonna owe the money jar when we reach Garek's domit."

I didn't know what he meant by money jar, but my mate was frightened, and I wanted to reassure her. I liked her here, pressed against my body. As did my cock. Unruly thing.

"Let me tell you about our eyrie," I said to distract her from the ground so far below us and my cock nudging her sweet ass. Her son was with us. I needed to regain control.

"Eyrie," she said, her head tucked against her son's back. "Back home, an eyrie is a roost for a bird of prey." Her voice came out thready but interested.

"We're gonna live with birds?" Noah exclaimed.

"I doubt it, sweetie," Piper said, sitting upright. She kept her head trained forward while her son pointed to this or that, exclaiming about everything.

"We live close to the trundier nesting grounds," I said as explanation.

"Where does something this big nest?" Her body relaxed, leaning against mine, and I was grateful her fear appeared to be leaving. Noah exclaimed about each bird and tree as we flew toward the mountains. He was made for flying a trundier. I would speak with Piper when the fledgling was not around. If he wished, I would take him to the trundier nests when the hatchlings were ready. No Earthling had bonded with one yet, but we ventured into a new world for all of us. If I could form a maelstrom bond with an Earthling, anything was possible.

"Perhaps you would like your own trundier?" I said to Piper as I directed Veskar in line behind the others. It was my job as warlord of my clan to provide coverage of the rear.

"Do women ride them?" she asked with a hint of interest in her voice. "I can't believe I'm saying this. Ten seconds ago, I was ready to insist you land so I could walk."

"And now?"

"It's…okay. As long as I don't look at the ground."

"Flying shows you the world," I said.

"You make it sound wonderful, but I'm going to need some time to adjust."

"We'll fly many sunslices. Will that give you the time you need?"

"Maybe."

"To answer your question, yes females ride trundiers."

As if to prove the point, Meriwee dove her trundier down, breaking formation from the others, then swooped back up to rejoin the group. Savvy and one of Alexa's twin boys rode with her, and both younglings squealed in excitement.

"Meriwee seems to be different than most women," she said.

"She is." I loved seeing her happy. She had too few female friends now, and I could tell she was lonely. I hoped she'd find females to be close with among the Earthlings.

"I'd think Ferlaern women would be too busy doing…whatever it is they do in your clan."

"In the past, our females would prepare the meals, tend the gardens and younglings, and comfort the males."

"Comfort, huh?" There was no missing the irony in her voice.

"Do you not wish to comfort a mate?"

My cock wanted comfort, the warm rush of her body opening to mine. It twitched, and by the way her back tightened, she felt it.

"Don't get…get…" She stroked her son's shoulder and pointed to a flight of blue-winged justiers flying below us, their four wings slowly flapping. "No hanky panky back there, Garek."

Noah chattered about the trundiers ahead of us, the birds, the mountains, and how awesome it was to ride Veskar, oblivious to our conversation.

"What is this panky?" I asked, intrigued.

"Panky involves this," she said pertly, wiggling her ass against my cock.

I groaned and my cock grew more rigid. My culier strands twitched and hummed. "Fuck."

"Now Garek owes the money jar," Noah said, lifting his arms in the air. "This is so cool! I want to ride a trundier for the rest of my life." He pointed down again. "Look, a river!"

"We're both in trouble." Her laughter snorted out, and mine joined in. "Are all you guys this horny?"

Horny… "Ah, horny. Yes. We each have two horns. We are all horny."

"I wanna be horny, too," Noah cried.

Piper tipped her head back and her belly-shaking laughter trilled around us. Her head fell back on my shoulder and she remained there, one arm around Noah, the other hand loosening on my thigh. I swore my powldron warmed to her, too. It tingled where the underside worked its way beneath my skin.

"Thank you," she said. "I needed a good laugh."

"Horny does not refer to horns," I said softly.

"It sure doesn't."

"It refers to cocks." I kept my voice low so Noah wouldn't hear.

"Yeah, it does. It's okay. This is an intimate position. But since you brought it up, I like your horns. Does that make me horny?" She snickered.

"Perhaps. And thank you. I like my horns, too."

"You said we have to travel many…sunslices? I

assume a sunslice is what we call a day, meaning from when the sun rises to when it sets."

"Yes. We'll travel for many sunslices but all of this…day. Rest if you want. I will watch and keep you and your son safe until it's time to land for the night."

"Where will that be?"

"Partway across this mountain range. We will cross three ranges like this one before we reach the one with our eyrie."

"Why so far away from where we're building?"

"We used to live in this region but many cycles ago, the duskhorde started encroaching on our territory. As they lived in a wasteland, we allowed them passage, eager to share the fruits of our world with what we hoped would be brothers. But they attacked and killed many. About that time, we discovered we could bond with trundiers, so we moved to where they nested."

"You knew the duskhorde would be in this area?"

"They moved on four or five cycles ago. We assumed they wouldn't return to your valley. Otherwise, we would never have allowed you to settle there."

"If only they stayed away." Her voice came out hollow, sad. She sucked in a deep breath and released it. "I really appreciate all you've done for us so far. We'd be lost without you."

Just as I was realizing I'd be lost without her.

I might tell myself I didn't want a maelstrom mate, but the fates gave one to me regardless. I would be foolish to deny her, to deny this bond growing between us. Was it possible to have everything I dreamed of plus her? I would speak with the elders. The notion that a warlord would push aside his duties if he formed a maelstrom was ridiculous.

I would never endanger my clan.

14

Piper

"You started to tell me about the eyrie but didn't finish," I said, curious about where—and how—he lived.

Noah slept in my arms. We'd flown for hours, and Noah finally stopped exclaiming about everything below us. I finally stopped gulping about the height. Never thought I'd say it, but I was adjusting. Sure, I'd be grateful once my feet were solidly on the ground, but I was doing okay.

This world was awe-inspiring; no wonder my boy couldn't get enough of it.

We traveled over a long series of mountains, and I couldn't stop staring at the lush vegetation and craggy peaks ahead of us. Despite relaxing, I avoided looking down.

"The Suthen Clan has lived below the trundier since we left the mountain region near where you hoped to build your new feral west," he said.

Feral must be a translator thing. I could correct

him, but I kinda liked it. The "feral west" had a nice ring to it and this place sure was feral.

Wait. "You said you live *below* the trundier?" I hoped they didn't lean over their nests and poop.

"High in the Woondral mountain range there's a series of broad valleys that are home to a species of trees not seen elsewhere on Ferlaern. They're big trees."

"Big is a relative term here. Look at you guys; you've got to be seven three or four. You seem to be… big all over."

"We are big," he said with a puff of pride. "But the trees are bigger."

"I can't imagine."

"You will see within a few sunslices."

"Will we travel overnight?"

"No. There are…"

"Let me guess. Predators bigger than Veskar."

"Sometimes."

"Lovely. Do they eat us, too?"

"Not so far."

"So, we need to avoid the big…predators," I said.

"We will be safe on the ground overnight."

"Anything big down there?"

He chuckled. "Just me."

While I was curious about everything around us, I also wanted to see what his cock looked like. I sort of saw it when he strode from the water, but I tried not to gawk and looked away. It was almost vibrating against my butt which was intriguing. It was totally inappropriate for me to be fantasizing about his dick, but there it was.

While we laughed about him getting a hard-on because my butt was pressed against him, the idea of him being turned on by me warmed something inside me. I hadn't cooled off despite the conversation or my fear of heights.

However… I was a mom. My son rode with us. Sure, I wanted to rip off my pants, lift up and ease myself down onto Garek's cock. Ride him until we both found complete satisfaction. It was crazy and spontaneous. I've never done anything like that. I was sedate. Boring.

Garek teased a different Piper out of me. She was nothing like the woman I was back on Earth. She was bold.

"All is well?" Meriwee said, dropping her mount back to float beside us. She flashed her tusks at me and nodded to Garek. "It is a good day to fly."

Garek dipped his head forward in acknowledgment.

Veskar flew up over the peak of a small mountain and Meriwee kept pace. We dropped down, and my belly flipped at our speed. I wasn't sure even Noah would find this fun.

Meriwee's gaze fell on my son, and her face softened. "So sweet. We are grateful for every fledgling you brought with you. They are our combined future, are they not?"

"Do you have younglings?" I asked. I wasn't good

at gauging age, but I'd guess she was about twenty-eight, like me.

Shadows crossed her face, and she turned her head to face forward. "No." With a shift of her feet, her trundier spun to the right and dropped down to dart around a series of tall stone spires.

"Did I say the wrong thing?" I asked.

"Meriwee lost her two fledglings to the disease," Garek said quietly near my ear. "She still mourns."

I'd mourn forever if I lost Noah. "She has a…mate?"

"She did. He was wounded while hunting in the lowlands last cycle and he died from his injuries."

"She lost so much." My heart ached for my new friend. Despite my crappy marriage, I could understand how sad it would be to lose a spouse I cared for. "Will she find someone new to mate with?"

"Perhaps."

The slight edge in his voice made me turn to look back at his face, but it gave away nothing. Maybe Meriwee didn't want to find someone new. If she loved her mate, she could still be mourning him as much as the loss of her younglings.

As the sun set, the trundiers drifted lower and approached a clearing.

"This is it?" I asked. "Home sweet home for the night?"

"We'll leave early in the morning."

A chill swept across my skin. "Do we need to worry about the duskhorde tonight?" Just the thought of them attacking again sobered me.

"We are deep within our own territory. They're not bold enough to come here, especially with so many warriors."

"Yet they attacked us last night."

"The Earth emissaries insisted on building in that area. We tried to dissuade them."

"Where do you think we should be?"

"In our domits with us."

Ah. Was that where this was heading? I didn't want to give up my dream of living in a new wild west. While traveling from Earth, I kept picturing a neat row of cute houses with flowers growing in window boxes and brightly painted doors. A covered market. And a big community center where we could gather. Squishing that idea into domits, whatever a domit was, made me feel like I was adrift in a stormy sea.

But the thought of living so far from Garek upset me even more. How could I reconcile my dreams for the future with him?

"We need to think about this," I said, not agreeing to anything. "Talk about it together."

"We will. Perhaps we can find a way to combine both our worlds? You had plans for your village. What did they include?"

I explained the layout I envisioned. "It's more than just buildings, though. It's what we'll do when we live inside them."

"Such as?"

"We'll hold parties and do fun things they did many years ago on Earth's wild west."

"You wish to hold parties?"

"Not necessarily. We want to have karaoke night. And play games. Hold square dances."

"Karee…" He shook his head, and his soft hair drifted across my shoulders.

I ached to touch it, to run my fingers through it.

"What is this dance of the squares?" he asked.

"It's fun. That's all. Fun." My shoulders curled forward as I realized my dreams were likely gone. There was no way we could make any of this come true while living in domits.

He landed Veskar with the others and slid down the creature's side then stood looking up at me. "Are you hungry?"

"Yes." Not just for food. I should be running in the opposite direction but instead, I wanted to leap down, wrap my legs around him, and kiss him. My lips still tingled from the last time we kissed.

Fuck. I was a goner. It was scary—and exhilarating.

"Time to wake up, sweetie," I said, rubbing Noah's shoulder. My son was the perfect distraction.

He stirred in my arms and stretched. "Are we there yet?"

"We're partway there. This is a…well, kind of a rest stop for the night."

He looked around and his spine straightened. "This looks awesome. We're camping again?"

"Maybe?" I wasn't exactly sure where we'd sleep tonight but like the domits, I would take things as they arrived and try not to worry about things I couldn't control.

"Cool." He slid off Veskar and into Garek's waiting arms. As he looked around, his face fell. "Do we have to worry about the monsters?"

"Not tonight." Garek lowered Noah to the ground, and my boy's feet churned as he ran to join his friends. He and the other kids started running around; to Savvy's displeasure.

When he held his arms out to me, I lifted my foot up and over Veskar's spine and slid down. Our bodies connected, and he held me as I glided down his front.

Yeah, he really was big.

Grunting, he stepped away from me. He unhooked our bags from Veskar and patted the beast's shoulder. With a happy huff—or what I took as happy and not, hey, I want to rip her head off before I depart—Veskar leaped off the ground and flew toward the forest surrounding the clearing.

"Guys," Savvy cried, trying to herd the wound-up kids. "Slow down. Please!"

One of these days, we were going to have to reward her. Like, with a castle. And a prince or princess when she was old enough to want one. A Ferlaern probably, but that was the local fare.

It was the only way we could pay her. Money was worth nothing here. How did the Ferlaern pay for things? I needed to ask. No, I needed a notebook to write down my questions and all the answers. Everything about this place intrigued me, but I didn't want to pester Garek with too many questions.

Okay, I kinda did if it meant being close to Garek.

Totally a goner.

"Where did Veskar go?" I asked, staring after the beast. "And will he come back?"

"He needs to hunt. Rest. And yes, he will return." Garek flashed his tusks, and that dreamy, swimmy feeling floated through me again. This guy's smiles were lethal.

As far as I could tell, I had two choices. I could float along and let fate decide where this went between us, or I could put on the brakes and slow it down.

Slowing things down was wearing me out. Back on Earth, I didn't date. Couldn't do that, now could I? I kept thinking, what if I ended up with someone like John again?

I was also tired of comparing every guy I met to my ex. I was savvy enough to know all guys weren't abusers. And you know what? I learned from my experience. I wouldn't take shit like that from anyone again. I'd fight back and deliver my own brand of hell to any guy who tried to hurt me or my son.

So, yeah, I was strong, but was I healed enough to start with someone new?

"Come." Garek held out his hand. "I imagine you'd like to eat and then rest like Veskar."

I might be confused about what I wanted, but my body was Team Garek. Dirty me wanted to ask if I could sleep close to him tonight, but I bit back the words. I only met him yesterday. It seemed reasonable to wait at least one more day before I dragged him to bed. Or to the leaves. Grass. Whatever substituted for a bed here at this alien rest stop.

"All right." I took his hand, finding it easier each

time he offered. We were slipping into something precious, something I shouldn't take lightly. He was one of the best things about this world. And for some wild, crazy reason, he seemed to want me. I could take what he offered or shun him.

His tusks flashed again and damn, that was sexy. I wanted to curl myself around him and… okay, rip off his clothes.

We walked over and joined the others.

I didn't let go of his hand.

A few of the aliens trudged into the woods and Garek went with them. They returned with wood and kindling for a fire. Since there was already a pit, it didn't take long to start a fire.

While others dangled a big pot over the flames on arched branches, Garek came over to me.

He held out a branch. "This is for you."

"Um, thanks?" I looked up at him but couldn't tell what the branch might mean. What if this was a dating ritual on Ferlaern? I could be missing the cue. Why hadn't the manual they sent gone into things like this?

"I have carried an oak, though we do not have oak. Oak translates to tree, however, so I have carried a portion of a tree."

There was more to this than I could figure out. "Double thanks?" What did the carrying of the tree—oak—mean?

"Now you have your carry-oke," he said softly, like he was giving me a great gift.

Carry-oak. Carry-oke. Oh, hell. Karaoke!

Okay, so this was cute and funny and sweet. I held my face tight because the last thing I wanted to do was laugh.

"Thank you for the sort of oak branch. Karaoke is singing."

His face drooped. "I do not sing."

"Not even a tiny bit? No swaying your hips while a perky tune plays?"

"No."

I sighed as if greatly put upon and held up the branch. "Then this is good enough for me."

He grunted, watching me.

What was I going to do with the branch? It wasn't sacred, thankfully, but I doubted tossing it on the fire would go over well.

Crossing over to where he laid our bags, I put the branch with our things. I'd figure it out in the morning after a decent night's sleep. Which I hoped we'd get here tonight. No shrieks. No burning everything around us.

I returned to the fire and stood with Garek while the Ferlaern males threw this and that into the pot. Soon, a wonderful-smelling soup bubbled. My belly groaned, hollowed out by hunger. They passed out bowls and I dropped to the ground beside Noah. He ate fast, like a voracious beast. Hell, I did, too, giggling with my son as we licked out the bowls. After, my son rejoined the other kids, zipping around the fire like banshees.

"Who wants to play tug of war?" Rayne asked.

Her daughter, Missy, hopped beside her, clapping. "Me. Me!"

Noah leaped from the ground and galloped over to her. "I want to. Please. Pick me!"

"We can all play," Rayne said, rubbing his shoulder. "Who do you think would win if we divided up into Earthlings against Ferlaern?"

"Duh," he said. "The Ferlaern are way stronger than us."

"Brains over brawn, though," she said with a grin. "But you're right. Let's see who wants to do it and then we can divide up into teams."

Noah skipped over to Garek and grabbed his hand. "Be on my team, Garek. Please?"

His sparkling gaze met mine, and his tail curled around my son's waist in a tail hug. "Of course, I want to be on your team." He stood and brushed off the back of his pants. "How do we play this tug of war? We will not battle, will we?"

"Nah," Noah said. "We take a rope, and each team holds one side. Then we pull. Whoever makes the middle of the rope cross the line first wins."

Garek rubbed his big hands together. "We have no rope, but I know of a vine that would work."

"I'll get it," Durran said, striding toward the woods.

Rayne watched him leave but then ran after him with Missy trailing behind. "Let me help."

Durran turned to face her. "The woods are not safe at night." He might not realize it, but his tail was coiling around her ankle. She noticed, and her grin widened. Aw. She lost her husband to the disease. On the ship, she told me she was coming here with hope in her heart that she'd find love again. Maybe with Durran?

"I imagine a big, burly Ferlaern warrior could keep me safe," she said pertly, though her face remained neutral. "I could find someone else, if you don't feel that's you."

"No!" He shook himself like a wet dog, and the scars on his face stood out in the firelight. What happened to cause them? "No." He continued in a more reasonable tone. "I will keep you safe but… Perhaps Missy should wait here with the others?" He stooped down to the little girl's level. At five, Missy was very petite. Noah's size and weight were off the chart, but Missy was the complete opposite. Tiny hands and feet and a slender body, she looked younger than five.

"I want to go," she said softly, shooting her mom a pleading glance. "It'll be fun in the woods."

"If you remain with the others, I'll bring you a surprise," he said softly and with so much longing in his voice, it cut through my chest. Yesterday, before the duskhorde attacked, I saw him playing with Alexa's twin boys, driving sticks through the air like space-ships. Later, he sat with Missy and patiently explained why the grass was blue and not green. This guy was made to be a dad. Would he get that chance with Rayne?

"What kinda surprise?" Missy asked eagerly.

"Wait and see." He straightened and barely looked at Rayne as if acknowledging her was painful. Was he shy or uninterested? Only time would tell. "Your mother and I will bring the surprise together."

"Okay. Just come back soon!" Missy pivoted and raced over to where Alexa's twins were throwing sticks into the fire while Durran walked into the woods with Rayne right behind. The tip of Durran's tail skimmed along her waist, though I doubt he noticed.

They returned not long later, dragging a long piece of vine. Rayne's face was flushed but her eyes shot fire—not the good kind of fire, either. What happened in the woods?

"Tug of war," she called out. The grim set of her lips told me she faked her enthusiasm. Uh-oh. "Come on, everyone."

We divided up with an equal number of Earthlings and Ferlaern on each side, then lifted the vine. Rayne dragged her heel in the dirt to create a line between the two groups, and we lifted the vine.

Garek took the spot behind me with Noah ahead. I was sandwiched between my two favorite males.

Two favorites? Who would've thought I had room in my life—okay even a bit in my heart—for anyone other than Noah? I decided now was not the best time to analyze it. *Go with it,* my heart urged. *See where fate leads.* Something I never would've done back on Earth but seemed to fit on Ferlaern.

"On three," Rayne yelled. She opted not to play and stood in the center as referee, studiously avoiding looking at Durran. I'd look for her later and find out what happened. I hated to see my friend sad. "One… Two… And Three!"

We tugged, everyone laughing. The vine surged forward, away from my group, but a grunt from Garek and some of the other males, and we stumbled backward.

"This is like your new feral west?" Garek asked close to my ear.

"It is."

"We carry the oak, and we tug this vine war. I hope this makes you happy."

Maybe I didn't need tangible things as symbols of the new wild west I envisioned.

Being with Garek and seeing Noah laugh for the first time in forever could be enough.

Our tug of war match was a draw. We gave up after about fifteen minutes of back-and-forth and decided to set up a rematch for the next night.

While Noah ran to play with the other kids who'd set up their own tug of war, I dropped my hair from its ponytail and gathered it back up to include the strands that escaped.

Garek teased one strand, tucking it behind my ear while I secured the rest. "Your hair is beautiful. Like flames and the prettiest setting sun."

This guy might be a gruff warlord, but he had a way with words.

He was slowly inching into my heart and taking over. Did I dare let him fully inside?

"Thank you," I said. I boldly tugged on a lavender

band of his hair. "Your hair is gorgeous. As black as night yet with purple highlights. Back on Earth, women dyed their hair various colors but never anything like this. I like it."

He beamed. "Thank you. This color is said to represent our ancestors while the black our future. A nice mix of both."

"It is."

Unsettled by his nearness and our new closeness, I scooted around him, looking for something tangible to distract me. A stream trickled along one side of the clearing, and I grabbed Noah and my bowls off the ground. When in doubt, do housework.

I *should* be safe at the stream. My gaze scanned the woods but other than the occasional swoop of a trundier overhead, I heard nothing I deemed threatening. I saw nothing eager to jump out and bite me, but who knew? This was an amazing world, but it was full of danger.

"Let me help," Garek said from beside me, taking the bowls I collected.

"You do dishes?" I asked. "If you can cook, I'm going to propose." Bold of me, but I couldn't help it. This guy brought out the woman I used to be before I was scared to be noticed.

"Propose what?"

He kept flashing his tusks. Which…could be considered a tad creepy. Why did I find it sexy?

Because I wanted him. No use denying that. Wanting didn't have to mean anything, did it? He wanted me earlier, when he had a hard-on while flying on Veskar, but it wasn't like we were sneaking off to rut in the dark.

Shit. I wanted to rut in the dark. Warmth pooled between my legs and I tried to shrug it off. Useless. My brain had been teasing my body all day with memories of him emerging from the water, a vision in burnished gold. And his cock…

"Proposing is…offering someone a serious relationship," I quipped. I was so brazen; you'd think I drank alcohol. What did they put in that soup?

The plates on his face softened. "Is that what you are doing?"

Well, um… Was I?

Suddenly shy, I scooted around him and gathered more bowls. "Time to head to the stream."

"Piper," he said softly as he joined me on the narrow trail weaving through tall, blue grass. Their seedpods whispered together, nudged into each other by the wind. The two moons had risen and lit up the evening just enough I could see where I placed my feet. "Did you mean that?"

Did I? "Maybe."

"Just maybe?"

It would be wrong to jerk him around. I shouldn't tease if I didn't plan to follow through. Confusion spilled through me, and I didn't know what to say.

"When we reach my domit, we will talk," he finally said.

I nodded, hoping I'd have something to say in reply.

We dropped to our knees by the stream and

started to wash the dishes. He scrubbed hard, lifting them up to view them in the firelight, ensuring not a speck of food was left behind before setting them carefully on the grassy shore behind us.

"You missed a spot," I said, pointing to one of the bowls.

He huffed and scrubbed the bowl again.

I couldn't help it. He brought out something frisky inside me. "You missed a spot on that one, too," I said, pointing. Heat burst inside me all over again. I was playing with fire, but I couldn't help it.

I flicked water at him, meaning to hit his forearms but accidentally hitting his face.

He paused and frowned at the bowl he was carefully washing for the third time. His head tilted and he stared at me as if he couldn't figure me out. If he did, I hoped he'd let me know his thoughts, because I was still clueless.

Water dripped off his chin.

"That was…refreshing," he said. He flicked water, and because his hands were so big, it drenched my front. His big hands had big fingers. I noticed. Tried not to dream about them touching me.

I sputtered while he flashed his tusks, but when his gaze swept down my front while I played wet t-shirt contest, his laughter faded.

"Piper," he whispered. His wet fingers cupped the back of my neck, and he tugged me closer. His head lowered.

Feverish and wanting, I rose to meet his lips. One of his big hands cupped my butt and pulled me flush against him. Damn, there was his cock again, pressing against the front of his pants. Pressing against me.

While his tongue dove into my mouth, seeking, I whimpered. I wanted so much more. Needed it. But jeez, we were out in the open. Anyone looking this way might see us.

I pulled away but remained within his arms, looking up at him.

"We, um…" I said. My body thrummed, eager to drag him down in the deep grass and have my way with him. Let him have his way with me.

His nostrils flared like he scented my heat. I liked that he knew I wanted him.

With a grunt, he released me. "We…" Shaking his head, he rose to his feet and gathered the clean dishes. He waited for me to walk ahead of him, but when we reached the firepit, Rayne's gaze met mine and she lifted her eyebrows.

I rounded the fire to join her while Garek packed the dishes away.

"What's up?" I asked.

"If I know these guys, Garek's cock," she quipped.

I frowned. "What's going on with you and the Ferlaern? You skipped into the woods with Durran, but something changed while you were gone."

"Yeah, that's the problem. What's happening so far? Absolutely nothing. Unfortunately."

"Is Durran interested?"

"Maybe. It's too soon to know."

How long did something like this take? I met Garek yesterday and already knew I wanted him.

"I called you over here to talk about you and the dishwasher," Rayne said with a twinkle in her eyes.

"You saw us." Hell, had everyone else?

"Only because I happened to look in that direction. I don't think anyone else did." She grabbed my damp hands and squeezed them. "Are you serious about him? Because it's as clear as daylight he has the hots for you."

"I don't know. Maybe."

"Lots of maybes being thrown around."

"Speak for yourself."

"I think you should decide soon."

"It's true. I don't like stringing anyone along," I said. "We barely got here."

"And you like him. A lot. Amirite?"

"You are," I sighed. "I've spent too much of my life worrying and I've transferred that to Garek." For the past three years, I avoided getting close to anyone who might hurt me.

"Maybe you need to start living. Test the waters, so to speak."

"In what way?"

"Take a walk with Garek. I'll watch Noah." She grinned. "You don't have to do anything I wouldn't."

I snorted. "And what would that be?"

"More like what wouldn't it be." She shrugged and her gaze drifted past me. I turned to find Durran looking this way. When he caught us staring, he shuffled his feet and backed into the shadows. "Go have fun," Rayne continued. "Talk to him. Get to know him better. Then you can decide if you want anything more."

The thing was, I believed I already decided. As rushed as it might seem, I wanted to be with him. He gave me something I didn't realize I needed.

"Hey, Noah," Rayne called out. "Want to sit with me and Missy while I tell a story?"

"Yeah," he cried, running toward us with his little legs pumping. He barreled into my side. "Love you Mom. Love it here, Mom. I hope we stay forever."

I stooped down and held his shoulders. "Love you too, Noah."

He gave me a slobbery kiss, the best kind.

When Garek came up behind me—I felt rather than saw him—Noah tipped his head back and grinned. "Love you, too, Garek."

My son had been as solemn as me for most of his life. It hurt yet gave me indescribable joy to see him happy.

Garek ruffled Noah's hair. "Love you, too, youngling."

Rayne winked and took Noah's hand, leading him and Missy closer to the fire. They sat on a series of big rocks encircling the flickering blaze and she began telling them about "the moonlight unicorn".

I pivoted and found Garek so close, I could feel his warmth through my wet t-shirt.

"I…" I sucked in my breath and pushed it out with my words. "Would you like to take a walk with me?"

He tapped his lips with his thick index finger. "Is that a proposal?"

"Um…" No more hesitating! I sucked in a deep breath and pushed out the words with my exhale. "Yes, it is."

15

Garek

It would be wrong of me to make assumptions. Piper wanted to take a walk; nothing else. But the scent of her arousal hit me between my brow ridges and my cock surged upward, a solid bar in my pants. The culier strands elongated and quivered.

We strode toward the river again but when we had left the fire's light, I took her hand. Taking a right at the stream, we followed it a few munettes until we reached the forest.

She stepped into the woods, following a thin trail winding slowly upward until she stopped and turned to face me. "So, okay, this is bold of me to bring you here."

"I appreciate boldness," I said with a chuckle. My body raged for her, ached for her. How could I deny the maelstrom? I was no closer to figuring out what I should do. My brain said to put her aside, to follow the rules laid out for us ages ago, but my hearts wanted everything. I was being split in two and would need to decide soon.

"It's unlike me to be bold," she said. "Back on Earth, I was a wimp about doing anything that would draw attention. Caution controlled my every action."

"There is nothing wrong with looking before you hop over the trundier pup."

"Exactly." Her face softened. "Is that what we're doing, jumping before looking?" Her finger traced along my jawline.

"I'll hold your hand when we leap if you want."

"Garek," she sighed. "I think I'm a goner."

"Where are you going?"

"Wherever you want to lead me."

My maelstrom heart surged forward, straining to reach her through my chest wall. Unable to resist, I pulled her close and kissed her, claimed her. My hearts thundered, and my breathing grew ragged. Our mouths moved together, and I threaded my fingers carefully through her hair, savoring the soft, smooth texture of the strands.

I stroked down her back until I reached her lush ass and cupped it.

While she moaned into my mouth, I squeezed her butt cheeks. She pressed against me, writhed against me.

A crack in the woods made us break apart.

She gasped. "Is that sound anything we need to worry about?" she whispered, her attention focused in that direction.

I listened for a long while. "It was nothing. I will rip apart whatever comes near."

"I appreciate that, but what if it's a cute little bunny?"

I had a feeling saying I'd rip apart a cute little boony was the wrong answer. "I will growl and frighten it away."

She tweaked my chin with her fingertip. "Great answer." Her mood sobered fast. "I feel safe with you, and that's saying something, Garek."

"You never have to fear me," I vowed.

She gave me a nod then turned and continued down the trail. I followed closely, my hand resting on her lower back. Stroking her lower back. Heat thrummed through me, centering in my groin.

As my Clan traveled with the seasons, we often stayed in this meadow while the moons shone overhead. I walked this area many times. There was a beautiful spot ahead I would show her.

Moonlight flickered through the leaves overhead, and the sound of laughter and chatter faded as we put distance between us and the group. Walking in silence, we continued until the woods thinned and we reached the small clearing I found.

"Oh," Piper said, pausing before leaving the trail. "It's pretty here."

I took her hand and led her across the open area overgrown with dreslin flowers. "They only bloom at night."

"They smell sweet. Heady." She leaned her face against my arm as we walked. "Like you."

"I smell sweet?" I chuckled at the notion. "Males are malely. We are not sweet."

"Sweet can mean many things," she said with a wink. "And you are sweet."

We came to the pool I wanted to show her, a place where the stream widened and was deeper. A small series of falls trickled over glow-rocks on one end, and the rocks' luminescence filled the water.

"Are there dangerous creatures in the stream?" she asked. "Anything going to nibble my toes if I dip them in?"

"Only I will nibble your toes, maidling."

"What does maidling mean?"

"Sweet one."

She chuckled. "Now I'm the sweet one?" Her words came out flirtatious.

"I'm not sure." Frowning, I pretended I had to think about it before speaking. "I'll have to taste all of you before I decide how sweet you are."

Her breath caught.

"And no, there are no creatures in this water that will nibble your toes," I hurried to add. Had I gone too far? "I swam here safely before."

"Hmm. So, it's safe." She wiggled her eyebrows, and her hands went to the hem of her shirt. "Ever skinny dipped before?"

"I…" My saliva caught in the back of my throat. "No."

"First time for everything, right?" She lifted her shirt up and over her head, baring her upper body to me. A fine white garment hugged her breasts, but a quick snap at the back made the material glide forward. She shrugged it off then shimmied out of her pants.

"Piper," I said, my hands lifting. So precious and smooth. I had to touch her skin.

She shook a finger between us and grinned. "If you want to touch—or taste—you're gonna have to catch me." Spinning, she raced down the bank and splashed into the water.

My cock throbbed. Literally jolted in my pants.

"This dipping skinny," I said in a deep voice overcome with emotion. "What does it entail?"

"Taking off everything and joining me. You can add the dipping part when you get closer." Turning to face me in waist-deep water, she smirked. Her fingers trailed through the water, and she lifted it and splashed her breasts. Her nipples pebbled. "It's chilly. I need someone to warm me up."

I needed no more invitation than that. I nearly shredded my pants taking them off. The straps holding my weapons clunked on the ground around me.

"Holy," she said as I strode to the water's edge. "I saw before, but the moment was tense. Too much going on for a full look. You're gorgeous."

"I thought I was sweet."

"That has yet to be proven but if you come closer, I'll sample and let you know."

With a growl, I dove into the water. I swam across the pool until I reached her, then plunged upward, rubbing my body across hers as I rose.

She cupped my shoulders as I emerged and clung,

her legs going around my waist. I carried her into deeper water, my mouth seeking hers.

She writhed against me, rubbing her clit on my cock. Grinding against me until my gaze blurred and I saw only her. My eyes rolled back in my head as the bliss of this munette sunk through me. My mate. My precious female. What had I done to deserve this honor?

We kissed and stroked each other, and I couldn't help it. I ground my cock against her, rubbing it through her folds to the top then dragging it back down. My culier strands quivered, a few trying to reach inside her. The one at the base of my shaft grew longer, thicker. When I was buried inside her, it would stroke her clit.

"Piper," I said when I lifted my head. My voice shouted caution. "I have to stop."

"Why?"

"Because…"

"Is this forbidden?"

I growled. "Not at all."

"Then let me feel you. All of you."

"You're sure?"

She shifted her hips until the head of my cock poked her opening. "I want you, Garek. Is it wrong of me to say that?"

"Not at all, but I'm going to suck on your clit first."

She sucked in a breath. "Far be it for me to complain if you want to suck me first."

I carried her to the water's edge and up the shore

where I laid her on the flowers and kissed her. I stroked her breasts, unable to resist moving down to suck on her nipples.

She arched her spine and moaned.

I nibbled across her belly then parted her thighs. Her wet folds opened for me, glistening.

Fuck. I was going to come just looking at her. But not without a taste…

Scooting lower, I slid my hand beneath her ass and lifted her up to my mouth. A feast I would devour. I latched onto her clit and rolled it, swirling my tongue across it.

She panted and moaned while I sucked and licked, desperate to take in every drop of her wetness. She bucked against me while her head thrashed on the flowers. Their sweet scent drifted in the air, combining with the lush ripeness of my mate.

I slid a finger inside her, and her soft inner walls clenched tight. "Garek!"

"You are beautiful. Perfect." I feasted on her some more, taking special care to rub my tusks on her clit, scenting her. Claiming her while pushing two fingers inside her. She was tight. How would I fit?

My cock throbbed, aching with need. The culier strands whipped and coiled along the surface, as eager as my tongue to taste her.

She pumped against me harder, faster. My tongue swirled across her clit then alternated by diving inside her, joining my fingers.

"I'm…"

"I want to feel you come in my mouth, maidling. Gift it to me."

My fingers went faster while I nibbled on her clit.

She shrieked and fell apart in my arms.

I kept licking and sucking while she quivered beneath me.

"I… I don't know if I'm good for more than one." Her laugh came out low and throaty as her fingers stroked my horns. Highly sensual, her touching them made my pulse soar and my cock surge forward. "Actually, even one with a guy is as rare as pink unicorns."

My chuckled slipped out, moving against her flesh, and her breath caught.

"Actually…" she said with a husky laugh. "Damn."

Standing, I lifted her and carried her back into the water.

She rubbed against my cock, and my culier strands tried to poke inside her. When we were deep enough the water helped hold her up, I grasped her ass in both hands and held her steady while I drove myself forward, inserting the bulbous tip into her opening.

"Ah." Her face dropped onto my shoulder, and she bit down with her blunted teeth.

That was all the encouragement I needed. Pulling back, I pushed forward again, burying myself completely. My culier strands sought her soft, slick walls, gliding along them while I pumped. When they quivered and stroked, and the short one at my shaft hummed against her clit, her head jerked up.

"What's that?"

"Do you like it?"

"Hell, yeah." Her eyes closed, and bliss filled her face as I pushed deeper. The culier strand at the base of my cock stroked her clit, tweaking and tugging. "Oh, hell. Fuck. Yes. Did you have a small vibrator in your pocket?"

"My main culier strand exists solely for you, Piper."

She grinned up at me, her firelight hair a deep auburn in the moonlight. "Don't go sharing it, now."

"Never," I vowed.

I moved in and out of her, and our soft cries mingled, echoing in the small area. My second heart pounded faster than the first, and my powldronless shoulder pinched, but I couldn't stop to look. I had to have her. Claim her. Show her intense pleasure.

Sloshing out of the water, I laid her on the soft flowers again. I didn't stop moving inside her but lifted her legs up onto my shoulders. Her body lay splayed out beneath me. Need creased her face, and she bucked up to my thrusts.

My culier shaft rubbed her clit. The elongated nubs stroked her inner walls whenever my shaft drove deep within her.

Her body jerked beneath me, and she cried out.

I went faster, riding her as she came then bringing her to satisfaction all over again. She thought she only had one orgasm in her, huh?

Her hands clutched my arms, and her head thrashed in the flowers, releasing their heady scent into the air. Whenever I smelled them, I would remember this munette.

My cock grew stiffer and the culier strands wove around my shaft, making it wider.

Her wide gaze met mine as I shuddered and shook above her.

My crest peaked.

My hearts moved close together, fusing.

When she came a fourth time, I joined her, shooting my seed deep within her.

16

Piper

I had no regrets. Not even a tiny speck. I wanted him. I claimed him. And he claimed me. It was the most wonderful experience of my life.

Nothing like good sex to change a girl's attitude.

Garek stood and swept me off my feet. He strode back into the water where he continued to cradle me in his arms.

He kept kissing me, and it was amazing. I'd wondered how his tusks would feel against my mouth, but he took care not to hurt me.

Sparks kept shooting through my bones.

I was so gone for him, I wasn't sure I'd ever find myself again, and that was a tad scary. Maintaining my individuality had been vital after I split from John. He sucked me in so deep I felt I deserved whatever he did to me.

After it ended, I told myself I'd never drown in someone else again.

It wasn't the same with Garek. He didn't smother

me. With him, I felt free to be whoever I wanted. Somehow, I knew he'd accept the person I chose to be.

"You are thinking," he said. "Someone once told me that a thinking female could be dangerous."

"That's majorly chauvinistic." I massaged his shoulders and neck, and the silky strands of his hair tickled my fingers.

"I do not know that term."

His tail coiled around my leg, moving upward. Would it stroke me between the legs?

I quivered in excitement, eager to try whatever he chose to do.

"Chauvinistic means macho. Alphahole," I said in a thready voice. That tail…

"Macho and alpha are other terms I don't know. Will you tell me what you're thinking?"

"If I tell you my thoughts then I won't be dangerous?" I couldn't stop teasing him. Yeah, he was a bit alpha, but he wasn't lording it over me. I had a feeling he was trainable.

"I want you to tell me whatever you wish," he added.

"I'm glad we came to this pool." I ran my fingertips across his chest. Would he think I was weird if I buried my face in his neck and nibbled? "I'm glad we had this moment together."

"There could be more," he said with a touch of hope in his voice. "I do not know how but we will find a way."

Like last night, I felt like a cloud drifted over the

moon, blocking something I needed to see. "What does that mean?"

"Nothing. No worries." He kissed me until I forgot my unease.

We floated, our bodies nudging together.

"This is going to sound weird, but can we take it slowly?"

His tail stilled so close to my entrance, I thought I'd scream.

"It would be a challenge to slow this down," he said.

"You know what I mean." Turning, I teased my fingers along his jaw, and he nipped my fingers with his tusks. His tail began its upward movement again, the golf ball-sized tip gliding across my clit then dipping slightly inside me. Just enough to make me pant.

"Let's take it one day at a time. We have now." How in the hell was I able to think? I arched my spine and spread my legs further. His tail poked inward, gliding. Yes… "We could…Let tomorrow happen when it arrives." I jerked against him, my body humming all over again.

He nodded slowly while his tail drove me toward the edge of something wonderful. It pushed in then pulled out, then teased my clit before repeating the process. "Things don't necessarily work this way on Ferlaern."

How was I following this conversation? We have two things going on at once. While he seemed able to focus, all I could think about was his tail. I rode it, bucked against it while he held me secure in his arms.

I reached my peak and shuddered around him.

The soft, okay, a bit conceited smile he gave me made me want to smack him and kiss him at the same time. His tail left me, which allowed me to pay attention to what we were talking about. That tail was going to be my undoing.

What were we saying? Oh, yeah, that things don't always work out the same way on Ferlaern. Kinda figured that, but we were two individuals easing around each other, trying to find a way to fit.

"Are you saying that because we had sex, I'm now yours?" I asked.

"I hope you'll want to be mine, but no, that's not what I mean."

"Then tell me."

A shout in the woods made us freeze.

"Reality's back with a vengeance," I said in a hushed voice, my feet dropping down to the bottom. At least his tail wasn't shattering me all over again. I wasn't sure I'd be able to walk if he did it again.

I peered toward the woods but didn't see anyone coming. But then, we didn't have flashlights. We were doing Ferlaern au natural. Anyone could emerge from the trail.

Soon.

"Piper?" someone called, followed by "Mom?"

"Noah," I said, suddenly frantic. I scrambled out of Garek's arms and flailed to the shore where I rushed from the water and dragged on my clothing. I had no idea where my bra was, so I skipped it. It might remain here forever among the flowers.

Garek followed, his hand warm on my lower back. He tugged on his pants and re-strapped his weapons across his chest.

I started across the clearing.

Noah burst from the woods at a full run. "I was worried about you, Mom." He barreled into me and gave me a hug. "The moonlight unicorn story ended, and you were gone."

"I took a walk with Garek."

Rayne ran from the woods but stopped when she saw us standing together.

"Sorry," she said. She raked her hair off her face. "That bugger's fast. I hope…" Her gaze went to the water. "Anyway." She smiled benignly at us, though her eyes gleamed. She well knew what we'd been up to. Most of it anyway. Our wet hair gave us away. "Hey, Noah, how about we go back to the others and play a game?"

"It's okay," I said, taking Noah's hand. "We were just about to return to the fire."

"Can we toast marshmallows?" Noah asked as we started on the trail.

"No marshmallows, I'm afraid, but I do have a candy bar I can share," I said.

"Yay." Noah released my hand and raced toward the meadow.

I walked slower, the hum between my legs telling me I'd been well and truly fucked and that I wanted more.

Garek kept pace behind me, his intent gaze on my spine.

That's when I remembered he'd started to say something important. What had he been about to tell me?

Instead of offering us spots on the ground around the fire, the Ferlaern went into the woods and returned with huge leaves resembling flat aloe vera. They laid them on the ground and then stood back, grinning.

One touch and I groaned. It felt amazing.

I tumbled down onto it, and Noah giggled and joined me. We rolled around, nearly falling off, and I tickled him while he squealed.

When we stopped and lay on the soft, squishy leaf mattress together, staring up at the moons, we found Garek and a few other Ferlaern gathered around us. They were all baring their tusks.

"This is amazing," I said.

"Awesome!" Noah crowed. "I almost want to go to bed."

"Ha ha," I said, poking him in his side and bringing on more laughter. "You never want to go to bed."

"I'm sleepy. Flying is a lot of work!" He turned and snuggled against me and for one tiny second, he was my baby all over again. Then he giggled and tried to tickle me.

"What will we use for blankets?" Rayne asked

Durran. He'd slunk in close but the moment she spoke, he stepped backward. He was either repulsed by her or shy. I had a feeling it was the latter. "Hey, um, Durran. Can you help me select my leaf?"

Guessed that one right. I noticed Durran right away—his scars drew attention. But I also noticed the kindness in his eyes and the longing when he looked at Rayne.

I'd watch Missy for her if she wanted to take a walk with him sometime.

He nodded and started toward the forest again, like he felt the need to personally select her leaf mattress. She winked at me and skipped behind him. With Missy on her tail, nothing tail-like was going to happen, but I hoped they'd get closer.

"Teeth," I said to Noah. We all needed a solid night's sleep after the horror of yesterday.

"Aw, do I hafta?" he whined. "I like them fuzzy."

"Yuck. No fuzzies other than stuffed animals."

It seemed silly to worry about dental care, but we couldn't get a cleaning here. Our teeth were coated with a lifetime protectant, but after that, we were on our own. Flossing and brushing would make all the difference. Especially if our teeth were fuzzy.

I nudged his side. "Up."

Noah groaned but scooted off the mattress. I took him to the stream and we both did our teeth. After, I made him wash his face and hands. If there was time before we left in the morning, I'd take him to Garek's hidden pool and Noah could swim. He hadn't bathed since the ship and he was getting gamey. We trudged back to the camp under the watchful eye of three Ferlaern to find someone had laid lush furs on each mattress.

"Where did these come from?" I asked Garek, stooping down to run my hand across the fur lying on the leaf mattress next to Noah's. I'd sleep with him sandwiched between the fire and me.

"We bring them with us when we travel," he said softly. "These are mine."

As you were mine, his tone suggested but I was going to roll with it.

"Thank you." I stroked his arm, and my hand tingled like it had before we mounted Veskar. What did this mean? "Okay, Noah," I said, shrugging it off. More static electricity. "Lay down and I'll cover you up. This is going to feel amazing."

"Don't I need to wear my jammas?" His yawn stretched his mouth.

"Tonight, you get to sleep in your boxers." I helped him tug off his t-shirt.

"What about Garek?" His sly glance shot between us. "Garek doesn't wear boxers. He gonna wear jammas?"

"We're going to leave that to Garek," I said, my face hot. I kept picturing us beneath the furs, completely naked and entwined.

Noah's lower lip thrust out. "I wanna sleep like Garek does." His head tilted as he stared up at my Ferlaern lover. "What do you wear to bed?"

"Nothing," Garek said. His gaze met mine and I

knew right away he was picturing the same thing as me.

Just like that, I was feverish for him all over again. If we did it some more, could I work him through my system?

Eh…doubtful.

The thought that I might want him for a very long time should scare me but instead, I kept imagining us disappearing into the woods together.

"Lay with me, Mom?" Noah asked, sending that notion into outer space. He'd tugged his pants off and tossed them on the ground. I shook them out and folded them, placing them at the foot of his bed to wear again tomorrow. "Would you tell me a story?"

I scooted him over on the mattress and joined him, stroking his hair while telling him the story of Peter and Polly Peeper, a tale I made up when we lived back on Earth.

While he appeared to be tending the fire, Garek remained nearby, listening. I liked having him close and not just for protection.

Noah drifted to sleep and before I knew it, I did, too…

I woke sometime during the night and stretched. A fur lay over me, the soft, fuzzy edge tickling my nose.

Of course, I had to pee.

Sitting up, I carefully covered Noah before shoving my hair off my face. My elastic had come off. If only I'd thought to braid my hair before lying down. It must be a rat's nest already.

Around me, everyone slept. Well, other than a few

Ferlaern I spied walking the outer reaches of the clearing. Knowing we had guards made my heartrate slow to a normal pace. It reinforced my trust in Garek. He wouldn't go to sleep and leave us vulnerable.

I turned to find him lying on a mattress right behind us, shielding us from the rest of the world. His eyes were open, but sleep crowded the edges. He bared his tusks when he caught me looking.

His fur blanket was tucked around his bare chest and I couldn't stop wondering what he wore beneath, if anything. He wouldn't sleep naked with everyone else around, would he? I wanted to crawl under his fur and grope him to find out.

He knew my thoughts. I could tell by the way his eyes went from sleepy to smoldering.

I nudged my chin to the woods, but he couldn't know I needed to go the bathroom. Probably thought I wanted more action. My body heated up, telling me it wouldn't mind if he decided to crawl between my legs again. Damn, I was wanton.

After tugging on my sneakers, I crept around the others, aiming for the woods. Garek rose and followed. Sadly, he wasn't naked. He wore his pants.

I started down the trail we used earlier, though I had no intention of going all the way to the pool and stopped after a short distance.

"I have to pee," I said, waving to the denser vegetation around us.

He stood there, watching me.

"I have to pee," I said again.

"I heard. Yes. Pee."

I spun my finger in the air. "You can't watch."

His head jerked back. "Why not?"

My lips twisted. "Why would you want to watch me pee?"

"To ensure you are safe."

I rolled my eyes. "I promise not to fall on the ground while I'm squatting."

He stared at me for a long while before spinning to face the other direction.

He'd know what I was doing, but really. A girl needed to hold onto her dignity whenever possible. It was bad enough holding my undies to the side and trying not to splash my legs.

Maybe I did want a quick dip in that pool.

I finished and tapped his shoulder after hiking up my pants and securing them.

He took my hand and we started back down the trail.

A crack in the woods to our left sent me spinning in that direction, but even with the moons' slanted glow, I couldn't see anything.

"What was that?" I asked, my skin prickling.

He said nothing for a long while. "One of the guards."

"Moving in the woods?"

His hand tightened on mine, and he hurried me back to the clearing. After ensuring I was covered, snuggled against my son, he straightened.

I watched as he loped toward the woods, his hand lifted to signal one of the other males.

Sleep was a long time coming.

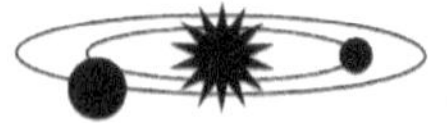

17

Garek

While I found no one during my thorough search of the woods, I did see evidence of a few people passing through. Thoughts of the duskhorde made unease travel down my spine.

Returning to the camp, I signaled for Durran and another clansmale to mount their trundiers and fly overhead. I waited impatiently until they returned.

"And?" I whispered.

"A small horde," Durran said. "Running. Think they caught wind of us overhead and bolted." He scratched his head, and his gaze drifted over the females sleeping by the fire, pausing on one particular individual. Rayne, if I guessed correctly.

I wished him luck there but only time would tell.

"Did you see any other groups?" I asked.

"I think they were a lone band." My friend, Bruge, shook his head and the deep purple bands in his hair shimmered in the moonlight. His tail thumped steadily on the ground behind him. The nephew of the Nulet

Clan's warlord, my friend was a highly respected hunter. Quiet, he hung back when others surged forward, and he expressed many times he was grateful his cousin would inherit the warlord powldron.

I glided my fingers across mine. I chose to wear it to bed as I had a feeling it was still fusing itself to me, the inner tendrils melding to become one with me. When I reached my domit, I would remove it at night. I was eager to test out its strength and see if I would notice a difference when I wore it.

"I'll take wing again and remain there," Bruge said. His intent gaze skimmed across the horizon where a hint of gold showed the sun would rise within a short time.

"Me, too," Durran said.

I tapped their shoulders. "Thank you."

After he and Durran left, I couldn't sleep. Instead, I strode around the perimeter, my gaze shooting to the woods whenever it sounded like a twig twitched.

***

"I can tell you worked a long time with Veskar," Piper said the next morning as we were preparing to leave. The leaf mattresses were dipped in the stream and laid inside the woods. They'd sprout new plants to feed the forest. Our furs were compressed and bagged, now hanging from our trundiers.

"Many sunslices," I said. "It takes at least a cycle to completely tame a trundier."

"A year? That's a lot of patience."

"But rewarding." The bond between me and Veskar would never unravel. "We'll remain together until he passes on. If he becomes too old to carry me, he'll be given a soft nest and lots of pampering for the rest of his days while I'll forge a bond with a hatchling and begin the process all over again. Trundiers live only one-fourth the lifespan of a Ferlaern."

Piper tilted her head, and longing came through in her words. "Can you show me how to be friends with him?"

"I'd be happy to." I was pleased she wanted to get to know my mount. "He won't bond completely with you, but I have a feeling he'll come to welcome you." To love her as much as I did already. Some would say my feelings came on too suddenly. Who knows? The fates have plans for us all, and we would be foolish to fight them.

"That would be great." She turned to call out to her son racing around the now-extinguished fire pit with Missy. "Hey, Noah, I'm going to spend a few minutes with Garek. I want you to wash up at the stream and do your teeth."

"Again? I just did my teeth and washed my face last night."

"Just like back on Earth, we have to do our teeth twice a day."

"We have leaves we use here to maintain our teeth," Meriwee said, coming up from behind to stand with me and Piper. "We chew them, and our teeth remain as they are." She flashed her smaller tusks that were just as perfect as her teeth. "If it's all right with you, I'll take him to the stream to wash and show him how to identify the leaves. They grow everywhere in the mountains."

"I really appreciate that," Piper said with a smile. Her face colored—a blush, I'd learned it was called, and I could tell she was happy to make a new friend in Meriwee. "Would you show me when Garek and I return? I'd love to chew some leaves myself."

Meriwee's warm gaze swept between us, accepting us. "I'd be glad to." She strode toward the others, calling out to the youngling. "How would you like to learn a few Ferlaern secrets, Noah?"

"Oh, cool," he cried. "Yeah."

"Let me get some things from my bag, and we'll go to the stream."

He paused and his face soured as if he sensed a trick. That fledgling was clever. "Will I hafta brush my teeth?"

"Actually, no. That's part of the secret." She placed her finger over her lips but shot Piper a mischievous smile over her shoulder. "I'm going to show you something that means you won't have to brush your teeth ever again."

"Awesome," he breathed. He raced to his mother and hugged her side while Meriwee waited. "Is it okay that I go with Meriwee? Please?"

"Sure," Piper said with a bubbly laugh. "Any time. She's a friend."

"Yay." He skipped away to join Meriwee. She took his hand and led him to her things. If I knew my friend, she'd show him how to find soap root while they were at the stream and ensure he was clean when they returned.

I turned to Piper. "We don't have much time before we leave, but I can show you a few tricks I use with Veskar."

She leaned into me and lowered her voice. "Thank you."

I put my arm around her, and we strode to the trundiers, Veskar lifted his head when we approached.

"When I first trained him, I taught him a signal and call exclusive only to me. Each of us do this. If you use it, he'll respond to you as he does to me." I assumed. Veskar could be finicky, however, but I hoped he sensed the bond between me and Piper and responded favorably to it.

"Do you still use the call and signal?" She tilted her head to look up at me and the early-morning sunlight hit her fiery hair, lighting it aflame. I'd never get over her beauty or the feelings I had for her.

How was I going to fix this?

"I rarely use it but I'm sure he'll still respond to it," I said.

She stopped a short distance from Veskar and turned to me. "What is it and what does it do?"

"If he hears it and chooses to respond, the call will bring him flying to you. The signal shows him you can be trusted. With time, he'll come to behave with you as he does with me."

"That sounds too simple to me."

I flashed my tusks. "All we can do is try."

"Are you suggesting he might let me ride him by myself?" she asked in amazement.

"Perhaps." I wasn't sure. Few trundiers allowed any but their bonded Ferlaern to ride other than as passengers. "Do you want to ride him alone?"

"Oh, wow. I don't know." Her nervous laugh skipped between us. "That's a long way up all by myself." A shiver wracked her frame. "Let's start with a meet and greet and take it from there."

"This is the call." Tipping my head back, I made the clicking-fluttering sound I created for Veskar when he was only a few sunslices old.

Piper frowned and tried it herself. "I don't think I've got it yet."

I made the sound again, and Veskar's ears twitched. He looked at me like he wondered why in the world I was calling him when he lay in front of me already.

She practiced some more until Veskar's curious gaze turned her way.

"That's it," I said softly. "You've got it."

Her grin lit up her features and made my two hearts pick up speed. "I do have it, don't I?"

She had everything; me, included.

I took her hand and curled her fingers into a fist with her thumb tight beneath, then flipped her hand over so the underside of her wrist faced the sky. "This is the first part of the symbol."

Her brow furrowed and she flexed her fingers, making the gesture a few times. "Seems almost too easy."

"Which is why it's the first part of the symbol but not the last." I took her hand and tugged her toward Veskar. "Let's get closer. I've never shared the symbol with anyone, and we'll block the others from view while I show you the rest."

"Kinda like a secret handshake, then. For one particular trundier."

I wasn't sure what she meant, but I savored the teasing light in her eyes. Was there time for us to sneak away before we left for the day's travel? A glance back at the others showed them packing things up, giving me my answer. Not this morning.

Maybe tonight. I craved her, though I knew my desperation came from fear I would be forced to set her aside.

Veskar rose to his haunches when we got close.

Piper's breath caught. "He's so big but I'm less afraid of him than I was initially. He's just a sweet guy, isn't he?" She held out her hand so he could sniff it, and he nudged her affectionately with his snout, bringing out her uneasy laugh. "Better show me the rest before he eats me."

"Trundiers do not eat meat."

"Somehow, that's not reassuring. Not with those teeth."

"He needs his teeth to dig the roots he enjoys eating."

"Tough ground then, because he's packing two rows of swords."

I chuckled. "One day we will watch them forage and you will understand."

She leaned back in my arms. "I like that. One day."

"I…" It was too soon to speak. I needed to keep my deepest thoughts hidden until I was assured we had a future. I ached to share my feelings. She deserved to know she was loved with everything inside me. I cleared my throat, cutting off the thought. I would settle this as soon as we arrived at our eyrie. "This is the second part of the symbol." Holding out my fist with my wrist facing up, I flared out my four fingers while keeping my thumb snug to my palm.

Veskar watched intently, probably wondering why I used a symbol I hadn't for many cycles. As I taught him then, he dropped to the ground, preparing to be mounted for flying.

"Whoa," Piper whispered. "Can I try and see if he'll do it for me?"

I flicked my hand up, and Veskar rose fully to his feet, towering over us.

She held out her fist as I showed her, then splayed out her fingers.

Veskar looked from her hand to me. He reached out delicately and sniffed her face. She held still, proving to me all over again how brave my mate was. Veskar stared into her eyes and I wondered what he saw, what he believed was happening. No one else used this symbol with him but me. He had to be confused.

Our bond was proven when he dropped to the ground and nudged Piper as if to say it was all right for her to mount him.

"Wow," she said. "I'm shaking. I wasn't sure what he'd do when he sniffed me but…" She turned and her eyes shimmered. "This is wonderful. I've had pets before, as I told you, but I've never had such a huge creature extend friendship to me before. I don't know what to think of it." Her arms went around me, and she spoke into my chest. "Thank you."

I held her, praying it wouldn't be one of the last times.

When Veskar looked to me, I could tell my own eyes shimmered. I nodded.

We left not long after. Noah asked to ride with Meriwee, and Piper agreed.

"I'm happy he's making friends," she said. "Me, too. I'll be honest, I wasn't sure how the females here would take our arrival. I hoped they'd welcome us like you and the other males have."

"Meriwee and I've been close for many cycles. I'm grateful you two are becoming friends."

"And Noah loves her already. He needs others in his life. For so long, it's only been him and me." She sucked in a deep breath and released it fast. "I want to tell you what happened on Earth and about my ex."

"What is an ex?"

"My former husband. I guess you could call him my former mate, though we're divorced. I don't know if divorce is a thing here, but it means a couple decides to end their mating in a legal manner."

"We have something similar here. If a couple no longer gets along, they can part." Maelstrom mates never parted. I wasn't sure it was physically possible.

Piper had sparked my second heart. It would not stop beating even if I set her aside. I would long for her forever.

"John—he's my ex. He was mean. Drank too much and when he did, he got meaner."

Anger surged inside me because I knew what she was about to tell me. "What did he do?"

"He was verbally abusive at first. But sometimes…" Her body curled forward, and a quiver shot through her.

I tightened my arms around her, wishing I could protect her from everything. But life had a way of slamming through us whether we welcomed it or not. I just hoped life would not deal us any severe blows.

I was foolish to hope this could work out, but what could I do? I spent my life working to achieve my goal of warlord and it was finally mine. Could I set that aside to be with Piper?

Tugging her back snugly against me, I kissed the side of her neck. "I'm sorry. I wish I'd been there to protect you."

"Thank you. So, John…" She rubbed her face. "Each time he did it, he promised it would be the last. I think after a while, he kinda believed he could follow through. He'd apologize then slip backward again. He knew I'd forgive him every time."

"Why didn't you seek a…divorce?"

"I wanted to, but he held all the power. I had a job, but it didn't pay well enough to save much. I hoarded what I could, hoping I'd soon have enough for me and Noah to escape. But then…" She quietly sobbed and I wanted to land Veskar so I could fully soothe her. I gave her the comfort of my embrace and hoped it would be enough.

I kissed her neck and shoulder and told her it was all right, that John would no longer hurt her.

"He hit Noah." The stark words rushed out of her, bursting through her tears. "And that was it. I could let him keep doing it to me, but I couldn't let him do anything to my son. I found the strength for Noah that I couldn't find for myself. I went to the police. They're the law enforcement on Earth. They arrested John, and it got dirty. He denied it, of course, but Noah testified. Seeing my son tell the judge what happened and…shit, Noah told the judge what John did to me. I thought he was asleep each time. Well, it kinda broke me. You know?"

I rubbed her arms and held her tight against me. "You did what you could when you could. You're strong."

"Eventually. I wasn't strong for myself at first, but I learned. John went to jail and I started a new life for me and Noah. We were okay. Things were good. Then John got out of jail and said he was coming after us." She lifted her hand and snapped her thumb and fingers. "Just like that, I was back where I started. Afraid. So, I applied for the Ferlaern program." Her voice lowered to something fragile and pure. "I didn't expect this, didn't expect to find you when I came here."

"I will keep you and Noah safe," I vowed.

Even if it was not at my side.

"I appreciate it, but I'm keeping us safe as well. I'll never allow anyone to hurt us again." She shifted around to partly face me and hooked her left leg up over Veskar. "This is going to be scary."

I swore mischief lurked in her voice, but how could that be? She'd shared something traumatic. I heard her break as she told me. Yet here she was almost teasing?

"What is scary?" I asked.

"I'm going to turn around while we're flying to face you."

Ah. "That will be easy."

"So you say, but I'm the one doing circus tricks mid-air."

Veskar swooped up a mountainside and soared over the peak. Below, a huge valley spread for what would be a long travel. We would stop for the night on the opposite side. Wind buffeted us from both sides, but Veskar held steady. A nudge of my heel told him to maintain this level, and he responded as he had from the first time I worked with him.

"I'll help," I said.

"Nope. I'm gonna do this one myself. Told you. I'm strong. Brave. Even when we're a bajillion miles off the ground." Her skin twitched. "Just watch me."

I released my arm around her waist so she could do it. She didn't need to prove anything to me. I already admired this female's strength. But she wanted to show herself something, and I would be here to support her through it.

Turning to face one of Veskar's sides, she brought

her other leg around and dangled them. "Shit, shit. Don't look down. Somehow, I forget how far away the ground is. Not so nice to be reminded of it now." Shifting a bit more, she slowly eased her right knee up and her foot past my abdomen. A flick, and she dropped her leg down Veskar's other side. "Hey." When she looked up at me, her eyes gleamed. "I did it! Just call me Houdini. Although..." Her head tilted. "This wasn't exactly a disappearing trick. But still. I don't know any circus performer's names, so Houdini it is."

"You are very brave."

She chuckled. "I bet you could do that trick with your eyes closed."

I had.

Her hand cupped my shoulders, and she wiggled forward until her body was pressed against mine. My cock responded, the culier strands humming. Closing her eyes, she ground herself against me. "I want you, Garek."

"We will land soon and be together." I'd find a way. Meriwee or one of the other females would be happy to watch Noah. My need for my mate was all-consuming; if I didn't have her again, I'd die.

"Hmm," she said with heat in her voice. Her aroused scent hit me in the brow, and my cock went rigid. "What other tricks do you have in your pocket?"

I reached down between us and undid her pants with a flick of my hand.

"Slick," she said, tipping back just enough for me to slip my hands down and against her skin. "Ahh..."

She pressed her forehead against my chest, and my hearts soared only for her. "No one can see us, can they?"

A glance forward showed we'd dropped back enough we should be clear. I could hold Veskar back further; the others wouldn't think anything of it.

I growled, wishing I could impale her. Removing our clothing while flying was impossible, but there was no reason I couldn't give my mate pleasure. I glided my thumb across her clit while pushing a finger deep inside her. "Come for me, love."

18

Piper

Knowing someone might choose to fly back and ask Garek something official should've made me scramble away from him. I needed to turn around and ask him to tell me more about being a warlord.

Hell, he should share whatever he was hiding. I could tell he was hiding something.

But I wanted him. So freakin' much. It was visceral and raw, grinding through me with no end in sight.

I rocked against his finger while his thumb played a happy dance with my clit. Shit, I was soaking my pants, and I didn't care. All I wanted—needed—was this moment with him. The world could go away for a few minutes, couldn't it?

"I'm going to make you come, mate," he growled in my ear. His lips teased down my neck. He nudged my shirt to the side with his tusks and bit the skin at the top of my shoulder, not breaking the surface but marking me as his.

When he slipped a second finger inside me, stretching me, I writhed against him. I didn't care if anyone flew by. All I could do was feel the wonderful joy this guy brought me.

The world slipped away, and my only focus was his fingers. His thumb. His tusks grazing across my skin.

Why had I thought I wanted to take things slow? Speed it up. Now!

I stuttered; my body overcome with heat. I bucked against him, not caring if I fell. Not caring if the world exploded around us. All I wanted was his fingers pumping inside me.

"Ah!" I rocked against the wave, and it swept me along with it, tugging me out to sea.

I wasn't alone. Garek was with me.

"Come, mate," he murmured. "Show me how I make you feel."

He pushed in deeper and captured my cries with his mouth. His tongue dove inside, mimicking the movements of his fingers.

I crested again, then my body took over, carrying me all the way to the stars.

Somehow, Veskar kept up with the others. Good thing, as we were a bit distracted there for a moment.

Eventually, I had to climb off his fingers and do up my pants. I pivoted around to face forward again and leaned into his embrace. His arms held me tight against him, and he kept kissing my neck. His fingers teased my breasts and whenever he stroked my nipple, my clit throbbed.

One orgasm was not going to be enough.

We still had more flying left to do, and when we landed, tasks would take over. Collecting wood. Making the meal.

I really needed to pay a bit more attention to my son.

But first, I needed a distraction.

And he needed to stop teasing my nipples. I did not, however, nudge him away.

"Tell me more about your domits," I said. "I'm curious. You said something about big trees and that you live beneath the trundiers."

"Yes." He stroked my thighs, which was just as arousing as his fingers plunging into me. "The trundier nest high in the canopy. Each spring, we return from the lowlands and resettle in our domits beneath. We gather fruits and dig tubers and await the hatching."

"What exactly is a domit?" I pictured a hut or something like the American Indians lived in long ago. A teepee.

"Domit means house or home. We make our homes within the blossom of the tree."

"A blossom? This must be a huge tree."

"One blossom is big enough for a family. They form in clusters and we open doorways between them. Then the younglings have their own sections."

"Huh." Sounded like camping tents with bubble rooms. The parents set up an air mattress in the middle and the children slept in 'satellites' hooked onto the sides. "Your clan migrates, then."

"We all do. Four clans live in our mountain range and each is led by a warlord. There are hundreds of Ferlaern in each clan, and each settle in one of the valleys high in the mountains. During the winter months, we migrate to the plains and gather. That is when we…as I have heard Earthlings say, party."

I snorted. My big burly warrior sounded so cute talking about partying.

My warrior. It slipped into my thoughts as if it belonged there.

I was ready. I wanted more. Should I tell him? Not while flying, but soon. When we were alone.

"What do your lowland domits look like?" I asked. "Are they blossoms, too?" I still couldn't picture how someone could live inside a flower, but I'd see soon. Within days—sunslices—when we arrived in the valley where his clan made their home.

"In the lowlands, we live on the ground in structures constructed from wuldra husk. The plant's broad leaves are impervious to water and easily woven into a tight mesh."

"Which do you prefer, the wuldra domits or the tree blossoms?"

He chuckled, his chest moving against my spine. "Both? Each is enjoyable when it is the right time."

I was curious to see blossom domits but equally interested in wuldra homes. Would I have a chance to see the latter? It was unlikely. We'd build our composite, Earth-like homes, maybe within his valley, and live there instead. Our new wild west. I couldn't let go of my dream, could I?

"Why migrate?" I asked. "I assume you travel based on season?"

"We return to the valley before the hatchlings are born. Long ago, before we discovered we could form a lifelong bond with a trundier hatchling, they killed us if we came near. If we are present the munette their shell cracks and they imprint our scent, we remain friends. Once the female weans the young, we take over and raise them as mounts and…do you have a word for a beast that is a friend?"

"A pet."

"Yes, we raise them to be pets."

I couldn't imagine a trundier playing fetch or sitting on my lap and purring, but maybe the babies are easier to deal with than the big creature I rode on. Cuter, too, I hoped. It wouldn't take much, not to disparage Veskar.

"How many hatchlings do they have at one time?" I asked. "I'm picturing a nest full of eggs and you guys scurrying around, trying to tame them all at once."

He chuckled, and the low, deep sound rumbled through his chest, vibrating against my spine.

It made me shiver in a good way. I really was a goner.

"The parents feed the young, but they only lay one egg every fifth season," he said.

"That's not many."

"There are more clansmales than trundiers."

"Like a wait list. How do you decide who gets the next hatched baby?"

"The trundier picks."

"I like that idea." I leaned back and his arm tightened around my waist. It felt wonderful being held by him. I couldn't stop dreaming about what it would be like to be married to someone like him, a kind, caring person. Not one who would hurt the people he supposedly loved.

We flew over a few peaks and in the distance, I spied what could be the domit valley.

Garek pointed, confirming my assumption. "Home in two sunslices." The longing in his voice echoed the emotion in me. Would I ever feel complete anywhere? I hadn't since I was a child.

After John was sentenced, Noah and I moved across the country. Since I was scared of what he could do even from behind bars, I changed our last name. We made friends but I never shared, and I cautioned Noah to do the same, to say his dad lived in Boston or Rome for all I cared. Anywhere but with us. That he didn't see him because he traveled a lot. When he got out, John promised to find us and make us pay—he left the message on one of my old name's social media pages. I logged in on a beater phone with data, refusing to leave a trail for him to follow or plant clues that could turn on us and bite.

As the sun set, we landed in another clearing. Tonight followed the same routine. Collect firewood and, as Noah called it, kindlin', then dig tubers from the bank of the nearby stream we paired with fish caught in the water. Others went into the woods and returned with leaf mattresses.

After eating, we lounged beside the fire.

Garek caught my eye, and heat burst inside me. I'd simmered throughout the meal, hoping we'd find a way to sneak off together. I shouldn't. I needed to maintain my guard.

But I wanted him.

I got Noah settled on a mattress beside me, and he was soon asleep. Riding on trundiers might not be much activity, but like any kind of travel, it wore a person out.

I stood and stretched. Could we sneak off now?

"If you would like to take a munette for yourself," Meriwee said, coming up so silently behind me, I jumped. "I will sit with Noah." Her soft gaze fell on my son. "He is beautiful. It warms me to be with him."

I could share my son. He had enough room in his heart for me and a billion friends.

"That's very kind," I said. "I'd love to stretch my legs."

"Then go." She flicked her hands and bared her tusks. "I will relax by the fire and watch him while he sleeps."

"Thank you." I strolled toward the trundiers with Garek right behind. It was doubtful we fooled anyone, but I didn't care. I wanted him and I didn't mind the world knowing it.

And that was a huge change for me.

When we approached Veskar, I gave him the signal. Like earlier, he dropped down to the ground.

"If I wanted to ride him, I'd just hop onto his back, right?" I asked Garek. Gosh, did I dare? The height could be dismissed when Garek's arms were around me.

His fingers glided down my spine, and I shivered in an amazing way. My skin tingled, and my clit throbbed. Oh, yes, I wanted him. I had a feeling I'd have him inside me soon, too, and that made my pulse thrum.

"Yes," he said. "Jump up and I will show you a few heel moves I use to guide him."

I clambered up onto Veskar's knee then leaped and grabbed onto the spike at the top of his spine. Somehow, I was able to wrench my leg up and hook my heel on his spine. Then it wasn't too hard to get the rest of me up on top of him. I surveyed the world —and Garek—from my new elevation.

As she said she would, Meriwee sat with Noah, her hand stroking his side. He was going to be completely spoiled by the time we reached our new, temporary home, and more power to him. My son deserved all the best in the world.

One jump, and Garek landed behind me. His arms went around my waist, though his fingers teased my thighs before they settled at my abs.

He leaned close, placing his chin on my shoulder. After a quick kiss on my cheek, he showed me the various heel moves he used to guide Veskar. I'd never remember them all, so I focused on the main ones. Fly. Go right. Go left. Land, please.

"Now you do it," he said.

A subtle tap of my heels at the same time, and Veskar's wings flicked out. He lifted up and soared off the ground. Eee… I wasn't sure I'd ever get use to being so high above the ground.

We circled over the others sitting beside the fire, then floated over the nearby forest.

"If you land in that meadow over there," Garek pointed, "we can dismount."

Fire burst through me. Shit, I was wet already. I could see where this was going. "What are your plans once we dismount?"

"I am going to fuck you until you scream."

19

Garek

We traveled two more sunslices. Each night, we stopped in meadows used by the Ferlaern for generations whenever we passed this way. We foraged for our meals and slept comfortably on broad chicalla leaves.

And after Piper and I ate and visited with the others, we sat with Noah until he fell asleep. My heart overflowed with love for the small fledgling, and I hoped we'd only grow closer.

Piper and I then went away together, leaving the sleeping boy in Meriwee or Rayne's care. We were feverish for each other, partly due to the maelstrom but also due to the feelings growing between us.

I'd fallen completely for my mate, but I still didn't know what I'd do when we reached the valley. Warlords were not allowed to form maelstroms. Could I find a way around this? Giving up my powldron would rip me apart, but I also refused to end this with Piper.

The afternoon of our fifth day of flying, we approached my clan's valley. Noah had begged to ride with Meriwee again.

"We're almost there, aren't we?" Piper asked.

"How can you tell?" I asked.

She snickered. "You're fidgeting."

"I do not fidget," I said, pretending affront.

"Then what's that leg doing?" She tapped my right thigh. "Keep it up and you're going to send Veskar in circles."

"Oh." I eased my leg away from my poor mount. "I'm…" I couldn't say it. Wouldn't say it.

"Nervous?"

I shrugged.

"Why?"

Because I still hadn't figured out what I would do. "I'm not nervous."

She sighed. "If you say so." Her breathing quickened. "Is it…" Hesitancy filled her voice. "About us? Are you having second thoughts?"

Fuck, no. "Not at all." I tightened my arms around her and dropped my chin onto her shoulder. I couldn't resist nibbling her ear, and she released a soft moan. One touch, and our skin lit on fire. I wanted her, now and for always. But I *was* nervous that something would tear us apart.

"Share with me?" she asked, an ache in her voice.

I wanted to but I didn't want to worry her. She had enough to handle already. Recovering from her experience on Earth. Coming to a new world to settle. Seeing her beginning settlement destroyed. Moving to another home. Raising her son. And a new relationship with me. I couldn't put this burden on her, too. I'd get it fixed and then tell her about it.

"There is something, and I will share it with you soon," I said. "It is not us." I kissed her cheek, wishing I could turn her in my arms and hold her—never let her go. I felt like I tumbled down a cliffside, unable to break my fall. I could only hope the fates would be kind to us, that they would help me find a way to make this work.

"You'd tell me if it was me, right?" An echo of past pain haunted her voice.

"I would and it is not. It's clan business."

"Ah." She sounded relieved. See? I was right not to burden her further.

"All will be well," I added. I hoped I was the only one who noted the concern in my voice. My spine crawled with worry, and I kept slowing Veskar until we were so far behind, my friends became specks in the sky.

Arriving later than the others would not stop what was coming, however. I did my mate a disservice by adding to the delay.

Leaning forward, I gave Veskar the signal to go faster, and we were soon riding at the tail of the others.

"I'm really curious about the trees you described," she said with a hint of excitement. "I can't imagine a blossom being big enough to sit in, let alone sleep inside. Do you mind if I continue to pester you with more questions?"

"Not at all." My words came out smooth. I loved that she was curious about her new home. She'd shared more of her plans for her new wild west, including the games she hoped to play in her center for the community, and I came up with something to make her happy. I'd ask the elders and if they approved, I'd share it with Piper. It was a way for us to combine our two worlds.

"Tell me more about the trundier," she said. "You said they nest in the canopy and you're there when they hatch. You bond with one and then raise and train it. How long do they take to grow big enough to ride?"

"Many cycles. They can fly within a few sunslices of birth, but they remain close to their parents until they are near the age to bear the weight of a clansman."

"And in the winter, you return in the lowlands. Do the trundiers come with you?"

"They do. By then, they have imprinted with someone and would mourn the loss of their bonded Ferlaern."

Her voice dropped to a bare whisper. "Do you think one would bond with Noah? He's so hopeful and I'd hate to see him disappointed."

"All we can do is try." I also hoped Noah would match with a trundier pup. It was part of my plan for our combined future. "I'll take him to the hatchlings. If the fates are kind, it will happen."

"I guess that's all we can do. It's not something to be forced." She shifted her hips, finding a new, comfortable spot. It would be nice to arrive home. We wouldn't ride again for many sunslices. "During the winter months, you hunt with the trundiers on the lowlands. What creature takes a beast the size of Veskar to bring it down?" She patted his flank, and he huffed.

"Nothing hunts trundiers."

His tail coiled around and stroked her shoulder. Each evening, Veskar carried us to our isolated location, and last night, Piper controlled the entire flight from mounting on the ground to landing. I was proud of how she took to my trundier friend and equally pleased with Veskar. They weren't bonded; that happened after hatching. But they were true friends.

"We hunt warslette in the lowlands," I said.

"They're big, too, right? Everything is here."

"Not so big we cannot kill them. Over the winter sunslices, we dry meat, preserving it for the rest of the year."

"There's no game in the mountain valley?"

"We only eat vegetation from the valley. The creatures there are for the trundier. The lowland plains host many herds of warslette. It's no hardship to hunt and dry meat for the warm season we spend in the mountains."

We approached the landing plain, the stump of a tree that died many ages ago. My friends landed and as they dismounted, their trundiers took flight, soaring toward the forest. They'd begin nesting soon and the air would ring with the chirps of hatchlings.

Piper leaned forward. "I don't see big flowers that look like homes."

"Soon." I pointed. "Look to the forest."

"Whoa. Huge trees." Awe rang in her words, and I was filled with pride. She would love it here; I knew it. And we would make this work, not just our maelstrom but her new wild west combined with the lifestyle of my clan.

"The valley's huge," she said, leaning back in my embrace. "It's bigger than the Grand Canyon back on Earth."

"We'll walk once we free Veskar," I said.

Veskar landed with a soft thud on the landing plain, and I leaped down onto the beast's knee. Turning, I reached up. "Drop, mate. I'll catch you."

A guttural shriek made me pause.

Elder Horesk stomped across the planed, wooden ground.

He sprang upward as he drew near.

Scrambling up Veskar's side, he slammed into Piper, knocking her to the ground.

20

Piper

A Ferlaern knocked me off Veskar. While he took the brunt of the fall, my teeth jarred together, and my shoulder hit the ground.

I flailed, kicking and shrieking, trying to get free.

Garek wrenched the other male off me and shook him. "Get away from her!" He helped me off the ground and nudged me behind him while pressing the tip of his short sword against the older male's throat.

Gnashing his tusks, the old guy pushed the blade away with his own and glared at us.

"Are you alright?" Garek asked me over his shoulder.

"Let me kill her," the old guy said. "We can end this now."

"It doesn't need to come to that," Garek said.

"What?" I cried in horror, backing away. The ground dropped off about ten feet behind me, but the valley floor wasn't far below. "Why does he want to kill me?"

The older male rushed toward me, his head lowered, and his horns extended to impale me. I dove to the side and scrambled to my feet, looking for a weapon.

Garek's tail stabbed out, tripping the old guy. He stumbled forward and fell to his chest. Lumbering to his feet, he raced toward me again.

I ran around Veskar to hide from the maniac alien, but Veskar wasn't interested in being used as a wall. He probably wanted to go hang out with his friends. Make some eggs. Avoid being impaled with Ferlaern horns. He took flight, soaring toward the forest without a single glance back.

"You dare too much, Horesk," Garek snarled, placing his body between us.

Evil dude's tail snapped out, aiming for me, and I stomped on it, grinding it beneath my sneaker.

The old guy wailed until I released him. Go ahead. Just try me. I wasn't taking shit from anyone.

"No, it is you who dares too much." Horesk said, his glare filled with pure hatred.

Garek shot me a look I couldn't interpret. My skin prickled. This was it. I knew it. This was the secret he was keeping.

I straightened my spine, preparing for a lethal blow.

"How could you do this?" Horesk flicked his finger at Garek's shoulder, pushing aside one of the bands holding his weapons to reveal a mark.

Creeping closer, I studied the small starburst

pattern on his shoulder opposite the powldron. I saw it earlier and assumed it was a tattoo or birthmark.

"How dare you form a maelstrom?" Horesk railed. "You wear a powldron!"

"What's a maelstrom?" I asked, dread coiling tightly inside me. I expected to snap.

I knew this was too good to be true.

Garek's chin lifted and his gaze full of sorrow flicked to me. "Piper is my maelstrom mate and I claim her."

"You cannot," Horesk said. "You wear this." He smacked the powldron. "Choose."

"I will not," Garek said stiffly.

"What does this mean?" I asked.

"A warlord cannot form a maelstrom," Horesk said with a sneer. "You can leave. We will discuss this."

"No way," I said. "First, who the hell are you?"

He drew himself up. "I am the elder of the Suthen Clan." Garek's clan? Great. Just great. Would I run into this guy all the time? "And you, Earthling female, have stolen."

I didn't like the sound of this. "Stolen what?"

"His future."

That sounded grim.

"Explain about the symbol," I demanded.

"When a maelstrom is formed, the couple will show this symbol," Garek said, his finger tracing the sunburst. His soft gaze met mine, pleading for understanding. Taking my hand, he squeezed it. "You are my maelstrom mate, Piper. My second heart beats only for you."

My chest pinched. I didn't know what maelstrom mate meant, not fully, but the realization hit me. I loved him.

"I don't have a symbol," I said. Releasing one of Garek's hands, I tugged up the sleeve of my t-shirt. My jaw dropped. "Hey, where did that come from?" I wore a matching symbol on my shoulder. If we had time to slow down and breathe, I would've seen it.

Garek grinned. "Maelstrom mate," he said with complete satisfaction. The joy in his voice made my skin tingle. It made me want to drag him away and remove his clothing, but we had to settle this first.

"Why is this guy," I nudged my head to Horesk, "pissed off that we're maelstrom mates?"

Garek's grin dropped. "Because warlords are not allowed to form true matebonds."

And there it was. My humor fled as fast as it arrived. "Why not?"

"You will distract him," Horesk sputtered. "End this or else."

I never liked ultimatums. "Or else what?"

"We'll strip him of his powldron."

"Can he do that?" I asked Garek. "You earned it. It's yours. You have dreams for your clan."

Dreams I refused to let him give up. My heart hollowed out because I knew how this would end. If he had to choose, it wouldn't be me.

"Unfortunately, he can take my powldron away," Garek said. He frowned. "Except…"

I wanted to believe he wouldn't let us down. That

he'd find a way for us to be together while still keeping his powldron, but how could I?

I struggled not to sag, not to give into mourning already.

Turning to Horesk, Garek kept hold of my hand. "I call for an elder high council as is my right as warlord."

Horesk hissed. "Very well." He scowled at me. "Meet us in the council chamber at dusk. This will be settled."

With that threat lingering in the air, he pivoted and strode across the open landing area.

I wrapped my arms around Garek. "He can't make you choose, can he?"

Garek kissed the top of my head. "I hope not."

"Mom!" Noah came racing toward us. He barreled into me, giving me a big hug. "That guy was being mean to you, Mom. Meriwee wouldn't let me come over here and kick him."

Meriwee joined us, and her hand dropped onto Noah's shoulder. "I felt you needed to get this settled without a youngling around." Her gaze went to Garek's maelstrom symbol. "So, it is true. You have mated fully."

Garek nodded.

"Congratulations," she said to me. "A maelstrom is rare but welcome."

"Thanks." I wasn't sure how to respond to that. While I was happy to be Garek's maelstrom mate—though I wasn't one hundred percent how that differed from a regular mate—this wasn't anything I made happen.

Fate. That's what Garek called it. Could I trust in something like that?

"If you two want to talk, I could take Noah for a bit longer," she said.

"I plan to take Noah and Piper to my domit, but thank you, Meriwee," Garek said.

"All right." She flashed her tusks and stroked my son's back. "Maybe another time, little fellow?"

"See ya, Meriwee," Noah said. He nuzzled against my side. "That mean guy better not come back. I'm a brave warrior like Garek. I'm gonna have a sword and a trundier, and I'll protect you, Mom."

"Thanks, sweetie." I stroked his hair off his face, realizing he'd need a cut soon. Or not. The Ferlaern wore their hair long. Noah would want to do the same thing himself.

Meriwee left with a lift of her hand, striding across the platform and down a series of stairs.

"Let me take you to my domit," Garek said. "We can talk?"

"Yes. We should." It hurt he kept this from me. If he spoke up, we could've come up with a plan together. Not that I understood how everything worked here, but if I was going to be a part of his life, that included decisions like this. I didn't want to bring that up around Noah.

My son chattered, half singing a song from Earth as we took the stairs to the bottom of the platform. At the base, I turned and looked up, gasping.

"Wow, that's a tree stump," I said. "A big tree stump."

"No, it's not, Mom," Noah said with a long-suffering sigh. "It's a landing plain for the trundiers."

Garek and I exchanged a look and despite how unsettled I felt, it was all I could do not to burst into laughter. Jeez, I was being boysplained.

"It was a tree, youngling," Garek said, ruffling Noah's hair. "But now it is a landing plain. You are both correct."

We started across an open field, sticking to a well-worn path cutting straight across. Noah skipped ahead, singing.

I slowed my pace. "Explain the maelstrom to me." My fingers traced the symbol on my shoulder. Why hadn't I seen it before? Well, probably because the only time I was naked, it was dark, and I was focused on Garek.

Frankly, as much as I needed to hear what he had to say, I couldn't stop staring at the forest looming ahead of us.

Veskar was big. Garek was big in many ways. But they were tiny compared to these trees.

"When a Ferlaern meets their maelstrom mate, their second heart starts beating," Garek said.

How could he talk when we were approaching such magnificence?

Wait. "Did you say two hearts?" I stared at his chest as if I could tell from the surface.

"Our second heart only beats when we find our maelstrom mate."

"That's kind of sad, but also amazing." And I made it start beating? "Do females have a second heart?"

"They do."

"Not me. Sorry."

He wrapped his arm around me. "Mine will beat for both of us."

That was swoony.

"I should be upset with you," I said. I was, but it was the last thing I'd share. I huddled inside, fearful. I'd watch to see how this turned out, but my hope for a future together was fading. How could he go against his clan rules?

"I would well understand if you were. Maybe you aren't because you love me?" He said it with such hope in his voice and I realized I hadn't told him. I barely acknowledged it to myself.

I gulped back the tears threatening to fill my eyes. That shadow was passing over me again, and it remained like a cloud heavy with rain. "I do love you."

"Mate," he breathed, stopping on the path. He tugged me close and kissed me.

"Yucky," Noah said. "Why are you always doing that? Kisses are yucky."

Despite my worry, I smiled at Garek. "You might like them someday, Noah."

"Never. I'm not kissin' anyone!" He spun and skipped down the path toward the forest.

"How long do you think that'll last?" I asked Garek as we followed.

"A few cycles still but one day, before we know it, he'll kiss someone."

We reached the edge of the forest and paused.

I tipped my head back, unable to believe how tall the trees were. "You live somewhere up there?"

"We do. You will, too, for as long as you wish."

The big question was: would we live together?

Funny how I came to this planet to start a new life for me and my son, never dreaming I'd include someone new in our lives.

Could I give up my dream for a new wild west to remain here with Garek? I didn't want to be parted from him but could we reconcile our two worlds so we could both be happy?

Of course, the decision might be taken from me. That thought dragged me back to the ground. He must've sensed my feelings.

"I will find a way around this." He cupped my face. "Do you trust me?"

"I do." For the first time in a long time, I put my life and my heart in someone else's hands. But fear was natural.

I was used to someone I loved disappointing me.

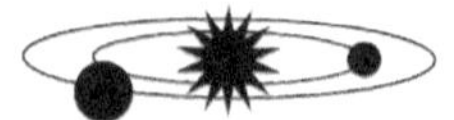

21

Garek

"Are you going to kiss again?" Noah asked with a sigh. "You're just standin' there. Aren't we going to your domit, Garek?"

"We're going to kiss again, but not this munette." I chuckled and took Piper's hand, leading her into the cool forest. A rich, spicy scent filled the air, the essence of the aresk trees.

She looked up. "Amazing."

"Where are your houses?" Noah asked, hopping beside us. "Will we have beds and a bathroom and a microwave?"

"You know there's no electricity here," Piper said, squeezing her son's shoulder. "But I'm sure Garek's domit will work out quite well."

Even I heard the reservation in her voice. It was hard to reassure her when I also worried. I hoped she trusted me to make this right.

"We'll…sleep on the leaves?" she said brightly.

"Even better." I tugged Noah close and wrapped my arms around them. "Are you ready to see my home?"

"Is it in the ground?" Noah asked with a tilt of his head. "I always wanted to live in the ground. Like a mole."

I had no idea what a mole was. "Not in the ground. We live in the tops of the trees with the trundier."

"Awesome," Noah said. He tipped his head back. "Way up there somewhere?"

"Way up there somewhere," I said. I grabbed onto a springer vine. "Hold onto me?"

Piper's eyes widened. "I take it there's no elevator."

"Even better," I said with a flash of my tusks.

Her fingers clutched the leather straps crossing my chest. Noah clung to my side and I wrapped an arm around him.

"Ready," Noah squealed in excitement.

One tug, and the vine yanked us upward.

Piper's fingers blanched. Her face blanched. I savored the way her skin could reveal so much of what she was thinking.

"Oh, shit, shit," she gulped out. "You remember I don't love heights?"

"So says the female who flew my trundier last night."

"That was different."

"In what way?" We reached the canopy and I

swung out, taking us to the entry landing. My boots clunked on the mesh surface.

"In every way." She pressed her face against my chest, and her eyes remained closed.

"Whoa," Noah said, releasing me to look around. "We're gonna live in a treehouse? Mom! Mom! We're gonna live in a freakin' treehouse!"

"Don't say freakin', Noah," Piper softly chided. She still hadn't opened her eyes. "Are we there yet?"

"We are here," I said, trailing my fingers down her spine.

She shivered and her lips twitched upward. "That feels good."

Just like that, my second heart thumped, and my cock twitched. The culier strands elongated, eager to glide against her inner walls.

If possible, I'd make her feel good all the time.

Soon. I would settle this and then we could begin our life together.

"Where do we go now?" Noah asked, his face alight with curiosity. He pointed with both arms. "This way or that way or up some more?" His feet twitched on the platform. "I want to go higher!"

"We're going to do everything," I said with a smile.

"Ha ha," Noah said. He tugged on my pants. "Where's your domit?"

I stooped down beside him, though I still towered over him even in a squatting position. "Look this way." I pointed to the denser area of the forest. "Do you see them?"

"I see big balls hanging from the trees. Like Christmas ornaments only they're dark blue, not red or silver. And they're way bigger."

"We live inside those balls."

He studied my face like I was teasing him. "Really?"

"Really." I straightened and held out my hand to them both. "Would you like to see?"

"Yeah," Noah said, his fingers engulfed in mine. "Are we gonna swing on more vines?"

"No, we will walk."

Noah peered over the edge of the platform. "There's no bridge."

"Oh, but there is." A tug on another vine, and a rope platform dropped down from above, connecting this section with the next. I waved to Noah. "After you, but no running."

He scowled. "Babies run. Boys…skip." His lips curled up and my hearts caught. He looked so much like Piper.

This youngling had stolen a piece of my second heart.

"Then skip, fledgling. But when you reach the other side, wait for us. I want to lead you to my domit. We respect others and do our best not to disturb them when we pass."

"You live in Christmas balls?" Piper said with laughter in her voice.

I was grateful she'd put aside her worry about what the elders would say about us. I sensed her overwhelming worry but there wasn't much I could do to reassure her.

"We live in blossoms," I explained.

"Blossoms, huh?" She extended her hand and trust filled her voice. "Show me."

22

Piper

He led me across the mesh-bottom bridge, and I did my best not to look down as we were hundreds of feet off the ground. If I kept my gaze trained forward, I could pretend I walked on a cute little rope bridge, one that brushed the grass below it. It wouldn't collapse.

And it was reinforced with steel. Lots of steel.

No steel in the trees. The bridge swayed and shifted, creaking with each step I took.

"You have an engineer here who makes sure the bridges are in tip-top shape, right?" I asked, my voice cracking with reservation.

"I still cannot believe you are nervous after riding Veskar."

"It's completely different." Though I wasn't sure how.

"We will be at my domit soon and you will not need to look down."

"I'm doing my best not to." And doing my best

not to think about the decision he was going to have to make. I needed to show him a united front, not cave like I ached to do inside.

We reached the other end of the bridge and I rushed forward the last few steps, onto another wide platform.

Noah held the rail and leaned over. "Whoa. It's awesome up here." He tipped his head back and pointed. "Can we go up there? I see something moving."

"That is the trundier's homes," Garek patiently explained. "One day, though, we may visit."

He winked at me. My heart filled all over again, but the heady emotion was clouded with worry.

He was going to choose his clan. I just knew it. It hurt when it shouldn't. Disappointment was part of life and if anyone knew that; it was me.

"Look down, Mom," Noah squealed. "There are little bunny things hopping down there!"

I was not going to look. If I did, the world would spin around me. I'd stumble and plunge to the ground. How was I going to live up here even for a short time? The elevator vines needed a strong arm to tug them. What if I pulled, it snapped upward but not far enough to get me to the platform? I'd be stuck dangling in the air until someone found me.

It wasn't going to work. Not even for one day.

I knew what my mind was doing to me, giving me an excuse to bail on this relationship before Garek bailed on me. I was afraid he'd choose his career. I couldn't blame him. He wanted to be a warlord for years—cycles. How could I deny him that achievement?

"You comin', Mom?" Noah asked, breaking through my gloomy thoughts. He and Garek stood at the start of yet another rope bridge.

"Sure," I said with a fake smile. Fake it until you make it, my mom always said. I sure did enough of that with John, pretending things were okay when they weren't.

I walked around the giant tree growing up through the middle of the platform and joined them at the rope bridge.

"Garek says that's his domit," Noah said, pointing. "Looks like a big bubble to me." He tipped his head back to look up at Garek. "Is the inside filled with balls like a bouncy castle 'cuz that would be awesome."

Garek's thick eyebrow ridge rose. "I do not believe it is."

"Huh. Bummer," Noah said. He skipped across the long bridge, and it rocked and swayed from his movement.

"You go ahead," I said with a wave. "I'm right behind." Actually I was going to wait until the bridge no longer shifted. If it was steady, I'd feel steady.

"Are you sure?"

I nodded; my hands white knuckling the railing.

He started across then turned back. Something on my face must've given me away, because he strode back. "Take my hand. It's going to be all right."

"I'm just nervous about the bridges." Mostly. I was also nervous about his meeting with the elders and what might come of it. It was easier to focus on my fear of heights than the idea that we might be yanked apart because of an ancient Ferlaern tradition.

"Want me to carry you?" he asked.

This could be the last time he holds me. "Sure." My voice croaked.

He swept me up and kissed me.

I drank him in like a cup of cold water in the middle of the desert. I wanted him for always, not just a moment. Knowing we might be forced apart was shredding me. It was all I could do not to cry.

"Hold tight," he said with a laugh.

I loved his excitement and because I didn't want to disappoint him, I plastered excitement on my face.

When he reached the other side, we came to a long strip of decking lined with five big, pear-shaped bubbles with small satellites lining the left side of the walkway.

"Which one? Which one?" Noah asked, dancing in place like a frenzied rabbit.

"The second one, youngling," Garek said.

While Noah raced that way, Garek carried me.

"You can put me down," I said.

"What if I like carrying you?"

"Then you should definitely do it." My voice was husky, overcome with emotion. Once he showed us around his domit, he'd have to leave. Would he come back or send someone to tell me it was over?

He wouldn't kick us out, but I might not see him again once he left.

We reached the second big pear. They were

uniformly shaped, and the outside was deep blue with white stripes gliding down the sides from the smaller top. Above that, giant green petals stuck out, absorbing the muted sun's rays filtering through the trees overhead. I assumed they also kept out rain. The domits were suspended from the tree like giant grapes, with long, vine-like stems. Each blossom was the size of a small house.

"This is amazing," I said.

He grinned. "Do you like it?"

"So far. I'm curious to see the inside."

"Then let me show you. It's open, Noah, just push the door inward."

Noah shoved it with all his might, and a part of the blossom glided to the side.

"How long do the flowers last?" I asked as he strode closer to follow Noah. "Do they fall off eventually?"

"Two cycles. This is the second for my domit. Before I leave for the winter domit, I'll select a new blossom and move my possessions." He ducked down and stepped inside.

"Wow." Noah stood in the center of the decent-sized room, staring upward. "There are stairs and another floor. Is that where my room is?" The hope in his voice surprised me until I realized he felt as homeless as me.

"There's a room up there or you can take the one to this side." Garek nudged his head to the right.

"Can I look at both before I decide?" Noah asked, his feet inching across the floor toward the stairs.

"Of course. The only room you cannot have is the one to the left. That is mine." As Noah scooted up the stairs, Garek leaned close to me. "I hope you will share that room with me."

"Show me?" I could keep dreaming everything would be okay for a little longer. "When do you have to leave?"

His sunny mood fled. "Soon, but I'll get you settled first."

"There isn't much to settle. Just a few bags." Which we wouldn't unpack just in case we had to move.

"I'll retrieve them from the landing plain and bring them here later."

How long could we keep pretending everything was going to be okay? My smile kept slipping, and I could tell by his concerned look he could tell.

He strode to the left and nudged the door flap to the side then ducked down and carried me into the attached room. A big bed made up of squishy leaves and covered with lush furs dominated the center. I could picture us lounging there on a Sunday morning —or whatever matched a Sunday morning here. Kissing, loving each other. Sleeping in each other's arms.

I wanted that dream so much. It was killing me to have it yanked away.

"I'll stay here with you," I said softly.

He spun me around, laughing, then stopped and kissed me until my head whirled. My heart was a furious creature in my chest, and I melted for him just like I did every time he touched me.

"Kissing again?" Noah said from the doorway. "Jeez. I like the one on the other side, Garek. It has a window, and I can look down at the ground."

Better him than me.

Garek lifted his head. "Later, mate." He lowered my feet to the floor and stepped back. "The room is yours," he told Noah. "I have to step away for a short time. Would you take care of your mother for me while I'm gone?"

Noah's spine tightened. "I always look out for her, don't I, mom?"

"You do, and I love you for it," I said, my voice choking up. He intervened with John, putting himself in the direct line of fire. I should've left John before it went that far. For that, I felt guilty, but I started to forgive myself. We did the best we could, and it was important to accept that. We'd try harder, and that was good enough.

I leaned against Garek. "It's okay if you have to go. I'll be here when you get back."

If he came back.

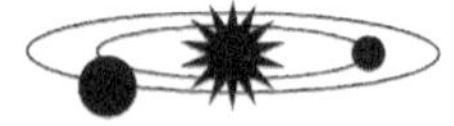

23

Garek

I ran into Meriwee on the walkway as I dropped the door to my domit into place.

"I was just coming by to see if I could take Noah on a tour," she said with a smile. "I imagine you and Piper would like some time alone."

"Tell you what," I said, bracing her arms in gratitude. "Keep him through the dinner hour and I'll owe you a big favor."

"No favor needed. I love spending time with him." She smirked. "And this will give you time with Piper."

"Exactly."

Piper tried to hide it, but I could tell she was worried. The best way to convince her this would work was to show her. The meeting wouldn't take long. Then I could return to her. Toss her onto my bed furs and follow. After I completely satisfied her in every way imaginable, I could take her higher into the canopy. Show her the stars and share my plan for our future together. "They're both inside," I said with a tilt of my head. "I won't be long."

"No worries. He's such a sweet youngling." She stepped around me and scratched on the door.

I left; my steps eager. This wouldn't be easy, but I needed to get it over with. I had a plan…

Me and my plans, but this one would work.

Soon, mate…

The elders' council chamber was in a tree on the opposite side of our village. It took me longer than I liked to get there. I scratched on the door when I arrived.

"Enter," someone called from inside. Narcial? Her input would be greatly appreciated. She wouldn't vote against me and Piper, would she?

I ducked through the opening and strode to the center of the large meeting room. The elders sat on cushions on the floor, each with a flask of sundair in front of them. Many of us enjoyed the spicy, chilled tea made from leaves harvested on the forest floor.

I turned slowly, taking in the twelve male and females dressed in ceremonial robes. How had they notified the other clan elders so quickly?

Horesk scowled, and I knew. He would want a full council to lend support to his belief I must choose. Their simple majority would decide, but he'd assume the other clan elders would not rule in my favor.

"So, Garek, you asked for an elder high council and we have gathered," Narcial said with curiosity alive in her voice. "Please state why you brought us together. I have not been told."

Interesting. So Horesk didn't bring it up to her already?

"I ask the elder high council to grant my plea," I said formally.

Narcial dipped her head forward, urging me to continue. The others watched, some with skepticism, others with scorn. Had Horesk spoken to *them* already?

"Enough," Horesk shouted. "There is no plea to state. You know the rules."

"We have not had a maelstrom mating in any of our clans for many cycles," I said, speaking to the others. Horesk had made up his mind already; there was no swaying him, but I had hoped the others could be persuaded. "Do any of you remember when the last couple formed a maelstrom?"

A few of the elders shrugged. Others stared at me with narrowed brows, waiting for me to finish.

I pressed on. "As you see, the powldron the Driegons found chose a warlord. Me." My back tightened, and I lifted my chin. I was proud I was proven worthy. They could not take that honor from me. "But the powldron is not the only reason I'm a warlord. I have proven myself worthy of this role."

"Your father should've passed his to you," the youngest elder of the Willen Clan said. "You are right when you say you're worthy. It was wrong of him to withhold this honor from you."

"You have proven you are qualified for leadership," another elder said, this a male from the Nulet Clan in the north. "Is this why you called us here? Is there a dispute about the powldron?"

"No," I said. "The dispute is about this." I slid my weapon's sash off my shoulder, revealing the sunburst pattern proving I found my maelstrom mate.

A few of the elders gasped.

"How can this be?" the Nulet Clan male said. "It's impossible. As you said, there have been no maelstroms for many cycles."

"This is why our race is dying out," Narcial said.

"We're dying out because of the disease," Horesk growled.

"Maelstrom matings always produce the most younglings," she said in a reasonable tone. She shot Horesk a stern look. "This you cannot deny."

"I don't deny it." Horesk rose to his feet and joined me in the center. He poked my shoulder, my sunburst. I kept my body rigid, unmoving despite his shove. "I deny his right to both. This is why you are here, fellow elders. He must choose as our rules dictate. He cannot remain a warlord as long as he has a maelstrom mate." Pivoting, he strode back to his cushion and sat. "Choose!"

"It would be wrong to deny a true mated pair," Narcial said softly. "But it is also wrong to deny the will of a powldron. This one is rare. I could not determine how old it is but see how deep blue the wood is? It was an old tree, a rare tree. A wise tree."

"The powldron made a mistake," Horesk sneered.

Narcial's brow ridges lifted. "You suggest I did not host the ceremony correctly?" She held his gaze until his dropped.

"This is not solely about more younglings," a

female elder of the Osten Clan stated firmly. "It is about traditions, the rules we have followed for generations. They serve a purpose."

"They keep us in line," I growled. "I have earned this powldron and the fates have chosen Piper as my maelstrom mate. To deny either is to go against the will of the fates."

"You would dare challenge our traditions?" Horesk gasped and I could tell right away he hoped I would take the discussion in this direction. "How can you lead our clan if you cannot follow the rules and protocols established many generations ago? You mock the elders who came before us."

"I do not," I said softly, bowing my head. "But I love Piper as much as I love my people. I can serve both equally well."

"I think you could do it," Narcial said. Her gaze swept across the others, and I was grateful they listened, though a few looked skeptical. "You have proven eight times you are worthy of being our leader in combat. Despite allowing Skydar to test the powldron first, it still chose you. Now the fates have seen fit to bestow a maelstrom upon you. Who are we to deny the will of the fates?"

"We interpret their will," one of the males said. "How can we say the rules they established many cycles ago are no longer worthy?"

"Who made this rule?" Narcial asked.

No one spoke. It had been so long, everyone forgot.

She looked up at me, and I tried to find a bit of

hope in her eyes, but they remained neutral. "Leave us, warlord, and we will call you back once we have made our decision."

I nodded and stepped outside.

"You may enter," Horesk said from the doorway to the elder's chamber sometime later.

I couldn't tell anything from his face, but it didn't matter. My hearts aflame, I followed him inside and walked to the center of their circle again.

"We have come to a decision, warlord," Horesk said with a happy grunt. "You must choose."

24

Piper

I dragged myself off Garek's bed where I'd fallen after he left. I wanted to imprint his scent in my mind so I could remember it during the long nights I'd face when we were no longer together.

Eventually, though, I had to wipe off my face—using water in a basin standing along the outer wall.

I left Garek's bedroom and strode into what was pretty much a big living room. I'd explore later if I was still here, but it didn't appear there was a kitchen. Did they eat together in a bigger blossom?

"Noah?" I called. Sitting with my boy would make me feel better. He was my past and my future, and holding him, playing with him would make my world okay. I needed to remember that we were the original team.

He didn't answer. Hmm.

I tried to shrug off my unease as I took the stairs. At the top, I found a small loft area with a hand-crafted wooden desk parked in front of a membranous window, plus a narrow frame holding one of the memory foam leaves. Essentially a daybed.

No Noah.

Back downstairs, I went to his room—his room for now, that is. Who knows what tomorrow will bring? We might be relocated in another domit by then.

I hated how discouraged I felt, how easily I assumed Garek wouldn't choose me. But maybe that was because I didn't want him to choose me. He was an admirable warlord, and he deserved this role in life.

Noah wasn't in the smaller bedroom either.

My heart skipped a beat, and fear took root inside me like a weed.

He wouldn't leave the domit without telling me. He might be eight, but he knew I'd worry, especially after what we went through together. We always told each other where we were going if we left, though Noah hadn't gone anywhere without me other than to the local park and then only with a friend and their parent.

I rushed to the door and flicked the blossom material aside. When I stepped out onto the walkway, I rushed to the bridge, but didn't see my son.

"Noah?" I called. "Noah!"

"Mom," his voice cried. "Help!"

I spun and stared in horror as a trundier flew in close to the domits. It hovered mid-air beside the bridge.

"Let me go," Noah shrieked, struggling.

Meriwee leaned around him, her stern gaze meeting mine. "Noah is my youngling now. Don't follow us or…" The threat rang in her voice. "Don't follow."

She whirled the trundier and they swooped downward.

"Mommy!" was the last thing I heard from my son.

In a flash, I was back with John and he was hurting us. I couldn't stand it.

I wrenched myself to the present. Just like then, my son needed me. I would not fail him now. My hands clenched the railing as Meriwee took the beast from the forest and out into the valley beyond.

"Hell, no," I whispered. I whirled around and nearly smacked into Rayne. Missy walked with her.

"There you are," she said with a smile. "I was just coming to find you. Thought Noah and Missy might like to play together. I found the most wonderful park up here. Can you believe that? A park in the trees."

"We're calling it a tree park," Missy chirped.

"Not very original of me, but there it is." Rayne's smile fell. "What's wrong?"

"I have to get him back. Noah. Meriwee took him!"

Rayne blinked fast. "What?"

"Noah?" Missy called, leaning around me. "Hey, Noah!"

He wasn't going to answer.

"Meriwee took my son. She flew away with him and told me not to follow or she'd hurt him!"

"Let me tell the Ferlaern," Rayne said, her calm voice filled with a thread of urgency. "Stay here. I'll be right back." She rushed down the decking with Missy holding her hand.

Like I'd wait here while someone else handled this? I ran across the bridge to the second platform then on to the first where I snatched a vine and yanked on it.

It whipped me up but then swept me downward. The ground approached in a rush, and I thought I'd plummet into it, but the vine stopped when my shoes were only a few feet off the ground.

Releasing it, I dropped, landing hard. I didn't stop but bolted along the trail, aiming for the valley.

I hit the open field at a dead run and kept going, my legs pumping, my lungs on fire. In the distance, I watched with terror as Meriwee's trundier flew up over the peak. She left the valley, taking my son with her.

Roaring across the big open field, I reached the stairs to the platform. I flew up them, my thighs burning and my heart on fire.

Noah. Please!

When I reached the top, I ran to the center.

Then I closed my eyes and made the chirping cry Garek taught me.

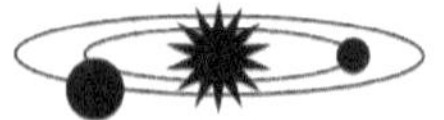

25

Garek

"You must choose!" Horesk shouted, nearly hopping in glee.

I did not hesitate. "Then I choose my maelstrom mate, Piper."

My words were greeted with silence.

Reaching up, I tucked my finger beneath my powldron and yanked.

It sunk deeper into me, refusing to release.

"What is this?" I cried.

Narcial rose and joined me, her face filled with sorrow. "See?" she said to the others. "We knew this would happen eventually." Her gaze returned to me. "There is no choice."

"What do you mean? Tradition says I must choose, and I have done so. I will remain with my maelstrom mate and forsake my warlord role in our clan."

"It isn't possible." She laid a kind hand on my arm. "Remember? The powldron picks the right Ferlaern and this one chose you."

"But I wish to be with Piper."

Her face smoothed, and she flashed her tusks. "You are the first. You will have both your maelstrom mate and your powldron and all that comes with it."

It sunk into me. "You lied." My glare swept the room. "All of you?"

"We carried on the tradition set by the original elders." Horesk burst to his feet and stomped toward me. "A warlord distracted by a true mate will not put the Clan first."

"So, you and those who came before you manipulated us." The horror of it clogged my throat. "All those warlords who could've been with someone they loved more than their own souls." Like I loved Piper.

"Watch him," Horesk snarled. "Now he will flit about with her and ignore his role in our Clan."

"He will not," Narcial said. Turning to me, she lowered her head. "I'm sorry. I played a role in this, too. It was wrong of me. But only a true warlord would sacrifice everything for the one they love, just as they would sacrifice themselves for the clan. Go to your maelstrom mate, warlord, and hold tight to her and your powldron. I cannot wait to meet her."

Horesk scowled but said nothing further.

"We will note in the scrolls that this rule has changed," the oldest of the elders intoned. "From now on, warlords will be allowed to remain with maelstrom mates if they are fortunate enough to form this bond."

Narcial nudged her head toward the door. "Savor your bond. It is rare and something to be treasured."

"Oh, I will," I said, striding to the doorway. Anger

drove my steps, and I didn't stop, but her words followed me out.

"Make lots of younglings. Rejuvenate our Clan!"

Outside, I halted and pressed my forehead against the wall. How could they do this to the warlords of our clans? I gnashed my tusks and fumed. So wrong. So incredibly wrong to deny anyone a maelstrom mating.

But… It was over. I would still need to process this, and I would tell Piper. I didn't own the elders anything after what they've done. What other traditions and rules did we follow that were grounded on something like this?

One of my first tasks would be to go through the list and examine them closely. Then I would call them together again and I would talk. They would listen.

I turned and leaned against the wall. Birds chattered deeper in the forest, and the calm of my village stole over me, sweeping away my anger and grief, replacing it with joy. I could remain a warlord and I would cherish Piper for the rest of my life. That was what I wanted to focus on now.

With my heart on fire, I ran for my domit. I couldn't wait to tell Piper it was over, that things were going to be, as she would say, *okay*.

When I was halfway across the village, I found Rayne running this way.

"Oh, good. Garek," she cried, rushing up to me. She panted but didn't stop to catch her breath. "You've got to help them."

"Help who?" Dread uncoiled inside me. Had

something happened to Piper? I gripped her arms. "Tell me."

"Meriwee took Noah," she huffed out, her breath coming in sharp pants. "Piper went after them."

"What? How?"

"I think on a trundier. Meriwee took him. How could she do that?"

Missy came running up behind her, tears streaming down her face. "You've gotta help Noah."

"I will, youngling."

I raced to a platform and hauled on a vine. When it deposited me on the forest floor, I bolted for the valley. There, I spied Veskar leaving the valley with Piper snug on his back. He was too far away to call back.

Fuck.

How was I going to rescue Noah?

A hum on my shoulder made me pause, and I stared down at my powldron.

Just like that, a plan popped into my mind.

26

Piper

"Faster, Veskar," I called, nudging him with my heels like Garek taught me. He responded, his wings flapping harder, his neck straining forward.

We caught up. Meriwee was only a hundred yards or so ahead of me. The one thing I noted when the duskhorde attacked was how handy Meriwee was with a short sword. I was grateful to see she didn't have one with her.

Noah strained in her arms, and I worried he'd fall.

"Hold on, baby," I whispered. "I'm coming."

Veskar flew up close, and I leaned over to grab my son. Meriwee hauled him to the side, and her mount dove down. They flew into a forest, and I followed, though my commands for Veskar were clunky, making his pace jerky as a result. But he seemed to know what I wanted and kept on the other mount's tail.

At least the trundiers weren't fighting. They probably wondered what we were up to; if this was a game.

As long as Veskar stuck with Meriwee's trundier, I'd find a way to free Noah. I wouldn't let her steal him.

We darted around huge trees, snaking through the woods. Branches cracked as we hit them and leaves were torn free, scattering to the ground below. Me and Viskar kept close to them, though how I didn't fall with the darting left, right, up, and down was beyond me. Thankfully, I wasn't someone who got carsick.

"Mommy!" A sob cut through Noah's voice, and it ripped me apart.

An ache shot through my chest. I had to get to him. Hold him. I fought to keep him safe, putting myself between him and John so many times. And when I hadn't been able to protect him, I left my ex. No longer staying around hoping he'd change.

I should've done it for myself long before then. I saw that now.

I'd save my son this time, too, and I'd keep him safe from now on. I paid my price. Life wouldn't ask me to pay again, would it?

Leaning low over Veskar, I clutched the spike and called to him. "You can do it, buddy. Fly fast. Catch them! Help me rescue Noah." My voice broke. Tears streamed from my eyes and were snatched up by the wind. I sniffed and dried my eyes. None of that shit. I could rage and break down later, once he was safe.

Meriwee's trundier darted up and burst through the canopy. I followed, branches whipping my arms and chest, and leaves smacking me in the face. It stung, but I shoved away the feeling. I'd give my life for my son.

I erupted through the tops off the trees and out into the sunshine. Veskar paused and I looked around. Fuck. Where did they go? Rustling treetops ahead gave me a hint, and I sent Veskar back down, into the forest.

There they were—ahead of us and not by much. I urged Veskar on, straining forward myself while giving him the signal to go as fast as he could.

A low branch approached. He was going to hit it.

I ducked, expecting to lose my hair when it was shaved off my head, but Veskar dropped at the last second and I sailed down along with him. My belly lurched. This was worse than a roller coaster, but we were gaining on her.

No more fear of heights. My single focus was my son.

Veskar nipped at the other trundier's tail, and the beast snarled. He slowed and spun, snapping out at Veskar.

Veskar roared and clamped down on the other trundier's neck like a lion would when disciplining a pup.

"I warned you," Meriwee bellowed.

Shit. She wouldn't hurt Noah, would she?

"Leave him alone." I reached toward them, strained toward them with my arms outstretched. "Give him to me, and I'll let you go."

I'd report this to Garek, but if she left the valley, she'd get away with attempted kidnapping and I wouldn't encourage Garek to give chase.

Her tail whipped out and smacked me in the side,

knocking the air from my lungs and nearly toppling me from Veskar. "He's mine."

The other trundier spun, flying up through the trees. Leaves and sticks rained down on us as Veskar took off after the other. I guppy breathed, trying to suck in air. The world swam and I thought I'd fall, but I kept a tight hold on Veskar's spike. My brain floated to the surface, and reality crowded back in.

Meriwee's mount soared up through the canopy with Veskar right behind. She flew over the rest of the forest then up a cliff face. Tucking to the side, she flew through a narrow passage between two mountain peaks with me close behind. I'd never give up. I'd chase them around the planet if I had to. Into the stars.

Yells rang out behind us, but I didn't look back. I needed to pay attention to Veskar's flying or I'd soar off and smack into a mountain.

She emerged from the passage and out into a vast plain that went on forever. Sandy soil stretched right up to the cliff but ahead, I spied a blue, grassy plain. Was this part of the lowlands?

I urged Veskar for more speed. He had to be tiring —her trundier would be, too. Desperation made me climb up onto my knees on Veskar's back.

"Mommy!" Noah cried, his arms straining toward me. "Please. Help me!"

As Veskar drew even with Meriwee's trundier, I nudged them closer.

Then I leaped from Veskar, toward the other trundier. I hit hard and grabbed my son, pulling him out of her arms while my feet scrambled for purchase.

She stared at me with her mouth open.

Yeah, never challenge an Earth mom.

She snarled and swiped out with her tail. It hit me in the side, and I tumbled off her trundier with Noah in my arms.

The ground rushed toward us.

27

Garek

When I reached the path to the mounting platform, Skydar was returning from a hunt.

"Call your trundier, Narle," I shouted, grabbing Skydar's arm as he strode past me.

He shifted the muskalier he'd killed and gutted from one shoulder to the other and glared at me. "I don't give a fuck what you want."

When he tried to shove past me, I wrenched him around. "Call Narle. I need him."

"Call Veskar," he snapped. "You don't need my trundier."

"Meriwee has stolen Noah."

That actually stunned him. He gaped at me. "What?"

"She took him from his mother and left the valley."

"Meriwee? She'd never do anything like that." He spoke assertively but his gaze didn't meet mine. A hint of deceit skimmed across his face.

"You knew." I shoved him. "You knew what she was planning!"

"Not all of it." His brow narrowed. "She's been mourning a long time, but I didn't think she'd do something like this."

"She has no reason to take Piper's son." The boy I'd grown to love. "He's not a toy to be passed around."

"She only wants to borrow him for a while."

"Liar!" I rammed forward, nearly impaling him with my horns.

With a grunt, he leaped to the side. The muskalier he killed dropped to the ground with a wet smack. Whirling, he plunged toward me, his short sword out.

I grabbed his arm, wrenched him toward me, then dove down so he tumbled over my spine. He landed on the grass with a heavy thud. I followed, dropping onto him and wedging my knee against his throat.

"Call. Your. Trundier," I growled. "Now."

He gurgled, his face darkening. Hate flashed in his eyes and I knew this would never end between us. He'd seek my weaknesses for the rest of my life and pounce the munette my back was turned.

"Let…up," he finally groaned. His hands smacked my leg, but I did not relent. "Let…me…up!"

"Will you call your trundier?"

"Yes!"

I backed up and off him but watched, waiting for his trick.

He scrambled to his feet and glared but didn't attack. Turning, he strode toward the mounting plain, and I followed, waiting for him to attack with my short blade out.

"I'm going with you," he said.

"I'll fly faster alone."

"Not on my trundier, you won't. I…" He gnashed his teeth. "I need to be there for my sister if you catch her."

I couldn't care less about Meriwee's feelings, but I relented because I did understand about caring for someone other than myself. Skydar was an ass but he loved his sister.

Two would slow his beast down. The munette his mount arrived to his call, I leaped up onto Narle and gave the command to fly.

The wretch remained on the platform.

"Release him," I growled. "Please."

"I go with you."

Frustration ripped through me, and I gnashed my tusks, my tail whipping, until I caught someone winging closer, approaching for a landing.

Yes, Durran.

Jumping off Narle, I waited for the other trundier to land then quickly explained.

"He's yours," Durran said, waving to his trundier. "You know he will carry anyone." As our head trundier trainer, his beast was the tamest with others. He could get the creatures to do things no one else could. Urgency filled his face. "Fly quickly, my friend."

I nodded and sprang onto his mount.

In a munette, I was winging after Piper with

Skydar at my side. Never thought we'd focus on one goal between is.

Would I be too late? I snapped and snarled. Pain arced through my chest, but my second heart beat true and steady. Piper still lived. But had she caught up to Meriwee and Noah?

"You know where she's taking him?" I shouted to Skydar. The wind of our passage sent my hair streaming behind me.

He only grunted and urged Narle to go faster.

We passed through three valleys without finding a sign of either of the females, then dipped sideways to fly through the mountain passage. Beyond lay a great plain, not the one we stayed in during the winter months as it was still too cold, but one we used for occasional hunting.

Meriwee and Piper's mounts flew close together ahead of us.

My heart plunged to the ground when Piper rose onto her knees. She leaped, and I almost couldn't bear to watch. She landed on Meriwee's trundier and they wrangled over Noah.

"Get close," Skydar said. "Take the youngling and Piper and get out of here. I will handle Meriwee."

Take them, huh? Easier said than done.

I urged Durran's trundier closer, watching in horror as Meriwee smacked Piper with her tail.

Piper tumbled off Meriwee's mount with Noah in her arms.

Fuck.

My powldron hummed, and I sensed it feeding me and Durran's mount power.

Banking to the right, we dove downward, spiraling while they rushed toward the ground.

I wasn't going to reach them in time.

Anxiety poured through me, and I clenched my teeth tight together, making my jaw ache.

"Faster," I bellowed, urging the trundier for more speed.

He flapped his wings harder, winging toward Piper. She cradled Noah with her body, and the terror on her face made my lungs freeze solid.

I swept closer as the ground rushed up toward us.

Reaching out with my tail, I snagged her leg and broke her fall then brought her close until I could wrap my arms around her.

As Durran's trundier banked upward, soaring toward the sky, I tucked Piper and Noah against my body. She sobbed in my arms with her son between us.

With my heels, I directed my mount back toward the valley, passing Skydar and Meriwee. Neither looked our way. Skydar berated his sister while she cried. Her gaze fell on Noah, and she wailed louder.

"Garek," Skydar called to my back.

I thought of continuing onward, of ignoring him, but until this—and he—were dealt with, it wouldn't be over. I urged my mount to turn then flew back toward them.

"We're not returning to the valley," Skydar said. For one munette, his gaze softened as it fell on Noah and Piper secure in my arms. "My sister and I will seek another clan and settle there. This…" His attention drifted past me, toward our valley before falling on my powldron. "It was never going to work."

I nodded then turned and winged home with my precious cargo secure in my arms, calling out to Veskar to follow.

"Thank you," Piper said, her voice muffled against my chest. "I can't believe you made it here in time to catch us."

"I will catch you every time, Piper."

She tipped her head back and smiled through her tears. "Always?"

"Always."

"I see you're still wearing your powldron." Her fingers traced across it and it heated, warming my skin.

"It is mine, as are you."

I said it like a joke, but she took me seriously. The sweetest expression crossed her face, and her lips curled up. "I am yours, Garek. Always."

Her arms tightened around her son until he wiggled and looked up at her.

"You came for me, Mommy," he said, sniffing. "So did Garek."

"Of course, we did," I said, flashing my tusks at Piper—no, at my maelstrom mate. The fates had chosen, and they picked wisely, gifting me with this precious female and her youngling son. "I love you both. Nothing will change that."

"The elders agreed?"

"After a little persuasion."

"Yay."

"Yay," I echoed. "From now on, we three are a family."

"A family?" Garek said in awe.

"That's up to Piper."

"Piper has already come to her own decision," she said pertly. The twinkle in her eye told me she wasn't upset with my presumption. I was prepared to back down if she was offended, though. I shouldn't push this in front of her son.

"And what has Piper decided?" I asked.

"Yeah, Mom, what have you decided?" Noah asked, looking back and forth between us. Hope bloomed in his voice.

"That she's where she belongs; in Garek's arms."

"Does that mean I can stay in your domit with you and Mom forever?" Noah asked me.

"For as long as you both want me," I said gruffly, overcome with emotion. "I love Piper, and I love you, too, Noah. You'll always have a home with me."

Noah's little arms wrapped as far around me as they could. "Love you, too, Garek."

"We're a real family," Piper said, kissing the top of Noah's head. She grinned up at me. "I love you, Garek."

My heart pretty much exploded with happiness.

My love. My new son. My family.

The life of a warlord couldn't get much better than that, now could it?

28

Piper

Two Weeks Later

"When can I look?" I asked.

"Not yet, Mom," Noah said. His shrill giggle rang out, and his fingers tightened around mine. "You can't see what it is! I bet you can't guess, either. But don't try because if you're right, I'd hafta tell ya and I don't want to."

I actually had no idea what they planned.

He and Garek blindfolded me—something that would be steamy-fun with Garek but was disconcerting when our son was involved. They tugged me from our home and were leading me to the "big surprise".

They'd been working on something for weeks together and our domit was filled with eager whispers and male bonding. They were cute together. Yeah,

Garek's job as warlord kept him busy, but the evenings were our time. After dinner in one of the domit dining halls, we went back to our own special blossom dangling from a tree. We played games, sang… Well, Noah and I sang. Garek stumbled through each tune, though his pitch was way off.

Tonight, they said they'd planned something special.

It was kind of creepy walking across bridges and platforms without being able to see. A test, I supposed, as I had become comfortable walking them with my eyes open. After my wild ride on Veskar, heights no longer scared me.

But blindfolded? I knew Garek would keep me safe but knowing one misstep could send me plunging to the ground kept me on edge.

Garek's fingers danced down my spine, and my nervousness was driven away by heat. Maybe he and I could sneak away from the evening activity and find some alone time. It was a challenge to find more than a second together with an eight-year-old boy around, though my friends were happy to babysit whenever I asked.

"Almost there," Noah crowed. "Don't guess, Mom."

"I promise not to guess." It was all I could not to laugh. I held it in because he was taking this seriously.

Garek did laugh, the deep, husky sound making me tingle.

This meant so much to Noah. To Garek, too. Even if it was more exciting for them than me, I would enjoy it. How could I do anything else when my two favorite guys were involved?

We heard very little from Skydar and Meriwee, and that was fine with me. They settled with a clan far in the west, one who lived exclusively on the plains and didn't travel to the mountainous valleys. They didn't ride trundiers, either. I imagined Meriwee and Skydar's beasts were a shock to the clan, though they knew we raised them. The Clans did, that is. I wasn't part of the loop yet, and still hadn't decided if I wanted to train my own mount if one chose to bond with me. It was fun riding with Garek, especially when we were alone.

I fanned my hot face at the memory of our last venture across the sky…

"We're here," Noah exclaimed. "Keep the blindfold on, Mom. No peeking!"

My laughter burst out of me. "I promise. No peeking. But you're going to let me see eventually, right?"

"Yeah, of course," Noah said. "Wouldn't be much of a surprise if you never saw it."

If he could see me rolling my eyes, I'd do it. Instead, I grunted.

We stopped and the hush of voices ahead made me curious. What did they have planned?

"Step inside." I could almost see Noah dancing around, his body wound up with excitement. "On three?" he asked Garek.

"Three…Two…and…" He tugged the blindfold off my face.

"Surprise!" everyone cheered. "Happy Birthday!"

"I'm not sure it's my birthday," I said. We couldn't exactly track the date.

"Sure, it is," Rayne said, coming forward. "Sometime around now. And for your birthday, we've created a new wild west here in the valley especially for you."

Aw. I looked around the inside of this extra-large domit.

"This is the market," Noah said in a chirpy voice. He frowned. "What are you going to sell here, Mom?"

"No idea, but if we can find a way to plant a garden and grow things in the open valley, we can offer them here," I said. "Remember? We brought seeds." They were packed away in our things and fortunately survived the fire.

"Like a food yard sale?" he asked.

Garek's brows lifted.

"A yard sale is where Earthlings sell things they no longer want," I explained.

"Why would you possess anything you didn't want?" he asked, completely perplexed.

"Sometimes you change your mind after you buy it."

"I see."

I could tell he really didn't. I'd explain later.

"Let me show you around," he said, taking my hand. Noah latched onto my other and they tugged me across the big open room. I waved and said hi to all my friends as I passed, Ferlaern and Earthling alike.

"See?" Noah said, pointing. "There are tables for your…wares. Not sure what a ware is but maybe the Ferlaern will want to buy it?" He released me and raced around the table, meeting up with Missy on the other side. They giggled and ran in the opposite direction.

Missy bumped into Durran and looked up, up, up at him. He bared his tusks, and she laughed before scooting around him. He turned and watched her chase after Noah with such a sweet look on his face I wanted to stride over to him and tell him someday, someone was going to love him for who he was not only on the inside but the outside. Garek told me he was shy about his scars.

Ferlaerns crowded into the room behind us, exclaiming over the tables, although I had a feeling they had no idea why we wanted them placed here. They'd see.

"Next?" Garek asked, tugging me toward the door.

"There's more? Really, the market is exciting enough."

He grinned, and his tusks gleamed in the low light. "Ah but wait until you see what else we have planned."

Garek was big on plans. So was I if they included me and him together. Alone. Naked.

We left the "market" domit and walked along the wooden planking to an even bigger blossom. A soft tune and the hush of voices reached me from inside.

"Tell me?" I asked, skipping back and forth on my feet. Excitement grabbed hold of me and hauled me away.

"That would ruin the even bigger surprise, Mom," Noah said from behind us. He scooted around us and raced to the door of the domit and swept the entry panel aside. "You're gonna love this even more than tables and wares."

"I'm not sure that's possible, sweetie." I stepped inside behind Noah with Garek's hand warm on my spine.

"Happy Birthday!" someone cried.

I really wasn't sure it was my birthday, but I was going to go with it. Everyone deserved a special day every once and awhile.

The room was bigger than the last and held more of my friends.

"Hold on, hold on," Rayne said from behind me. First, she tied a flouncy skirt around my waist then another on herself. With a chuckle, she raced across the room to a small table set along the far wall, her skirt flicking up in the air. Good thing she wore leggings beneath it. Her gaze sought Garek's, and he nodded.

"Any time, guys," she called. When her arms lifted, what looked like round brown balls puffed up in the corner, their fur standing out in all directions like they stuck their fingers—or toes, feelers, whatever—in a light socket. We had no light sockets here, so this was their natural fluffiness. If they were friendly and allowed it, I so needed to pat them.

The creature in the front lifted a few pieces of wood and started rubbing them together. Its simple tune was enhanced when the others did the same, lifting wood and gliding them together, until a perky song danced through the room.

"Hey everyone," Rayne yelled. "Let's gather round." She shot a giggle over her shoulder my way. "Come on, you, two, Garek's been practicing and he's dying to show you what he can do."

"What…?" I blinked, unable to take it all in. Some of the aliens tugged on red checkered…tunics and belted them at the waist. Garek stuffed his arms into the sleeves of a blue checkered one and secured it with one of his weapons straps. He looked…amazing. I'd never seen him wearing a shirt before as he preferred to keep his weapon handy. All the women donned skirts in bright colors, and most of the guys, checks. "What is this?"

"This is your dance hall, Piper," Garek said gruffly. "Just like you wanted for your feral wild west." He grabbed something vaguely resembling a cowboy hat off a nearby table and wedged it onto his head, his horns sticking up through two convenient holes in the front. Then he held out his arm to me. "Would you like to square dance?"

Someone hooted, and the sound was followed by other cries mixed in with laughter.

Big bronze aliens were going to square dance? I wasn't sure which I wanted to do more, laugh or join them when they stomped around the room.

I opted for the later, skipping out into the middle of the room on Garek's arm.

He whirled me around to stand beside him.

Rayne partnered with Missy, though she shot a longing look Durran's way. He leaned against the wall, partly hidden in the shadows. Did he worry she wouldn't want someone who faced something horrible and came up the victor? One of these days, he would see his heart would be safe with Rayne.

A Ferlaern male I hadn't seen before stepped inside. He wasn't dressed for the party. Instead, he wore a fur draped over his shoulders and cinched snug at his waist. He surveyed the crowd grimly before his attention locked on Durran. He strode around the outside of the room and up to the other male, and they spoke quietly together.

Durran sent Rayne a solemn look before he and the other Ferlaern left the dance hall.

"Ready?" Rayne called out, drawing my gaze back to her. Had she seen Durran leave? Shadows lurked on her face before she shook them off and smiled. "One, two, three, and four."

The puffy creatures' tune picked up, sounding surprisingly like violins, and I let my curiosity about Durran slide. Time to focus on the moment, not on what might be happening behind the scenes.

I grinned and bowed to Garek, then he swept me around with his arm around my waist.

"To the left then spin her 'round," Rayne called out. She swept Missy up and whirled in a circle while her daughter giggled.

One of the Ferlaern sang that Suzannah shouldn't cry for him. His voice needed work, but singing wasn't the norm for Ferlaerns.

"Circle to the left!" Rayne cried.

A few of the aliens smacked together, not exactly sure which was left, but they covered by twirling each other in a circle. One stumbled backward, his hoot ringing to the ceiling two stories above.

I hooked my hand on Garek's elbow and we circled.

"Ladies sashay into the middle." Rayne led us into the center of the circle, and we flared our skirts before moving back to the outer ring.

Shouts rang out, and a couple of the Ferlaern bellowed the refrain about coming from Alabama with a banjo on their knee.

I couldn't stop laughing. Tears of joy streaked down my face.

"Shoot the star," Rayne called out, and each couple formed the spokes of a wheel and stomped around until we became a jumbled, laughing mess.

We formed two lines and danced down the outside, swinging from one person to the next until we reached the end. Then each couple skipped down the middle of the two rows.

Some of the guys danced with women, others with each other. They kicked their legs, forming like a bizarre chorus line for a second before spinning around and wiggling their butts.

Garek took my hand and we sashayed down the center of a line of swaying dancers, their clapping driving us on.

When we reached the end, he lifted me up. He spun me around and when I slid down his front, his lips met mine. I clung to him, gripping his horns tight while his tongue teased mine, full of promise. I melted into him. I'd always melt into him.

During our journey from Earth, I fretted that things on Ferlaern would be too different and not be enough like Earth.

Instead, I found something better.

Noah couldn't be happier. He had a new dad, and if things worked out, his very own trundier pup. I was going to have a heart attack during his first solo ride, but I wanted him to feel a part of our new life, and this was one of the ways.

My friends were flirting with Ferlaerns, and I had a feeling my maelstrom with Garek wouldn't be the first.

And Garek…

Sigh. I couldn't love anyone more.

If I could send the old, Earth me a message, I'd tell her not to worry. She'd find her heart again. She'd be happy.

And I'd tell her that things were going to be… Well, as Noah would say, awesome.

Would you like to read a bonus
epilogue from *Enticed by an Alien Warlord*?
It's yours FREE when you sign up for my newsletter.
The trundier pups have hatched &
Garek has a surprise for both Piper & Noah.
Sign me up!

If you'd like to read Chapter 1 of *Tamed by an Alien Warlord,*
Book 2 in the Fated Mates of the Ferlaern Warriors Series,
turn the page and dig into
Durran & Rayne's romance!
Missy, Rayne's six-year-old daughter
is eager for an alien daddy.

If you enjoyed Garek & Piper's story,
would you leave a review?
Few readers do and
I'LL LOVE YOU FOREVER!
You can leave your review on Amazon.

About the Author

Ava Ross fell for men with unusual features when she first watched Star Wars, where alien creatures have gone mainstream. She lives in New England with her husband (who is sadly not an alien, though he is still cute in his own way), her kids, and a few assorted pets.

Kruze
(A prequel novella free with
newsletter sign-up)

IN LOVE WITH AN ALIEN ANTHOLOGY

Neere,
a Brides of Driegon short story

ALIEN EMBRACE ANTHOLOGY

Skoar
a Brides of Driegon novella

FATED MATES OF THE FERLAERN WARRIORS

Enticed by an Alien Warlord
Tamed by an Alien Warlord
Seduced by an Alien Warlord
Tempted by an Alien Warlord

You can find my books on Amazon.

TAMED BY AN ALIEN
WARLORD

He's shy and scarred and thinks no one will ever love him. She's determined to show him he's the hottest alien in the universe.

Durran: The Earthling females are settling into our clan, finding new homes high in the forest's canopy. Matches are being made but not for me. Scarred as I am, none will ever glance my way. But one Earthling... Rayne's sweet and funny, and I want to scoop her up in my arms and kiss her until she moans my name. To protect my heart, I'll keep busy with my investigation into a new threat to our clan. Someone's harming our trees, and I need to stop them before our way of life is destroyed.

Rayne: To distract myself from my ongoing lust for Durran, I'm focusing on researching the substance poisoning the clan's trees and raising my five-year-old daughter. She's bonding with a trundier, and I'm worried she'll fly off into the sunset on the creature that pretty much looks like a giant hornet. But when Durran and I kiss, and kisses lead to other things, I'm thrown for a loop. Can a gruff alien trundier trainer and a single mom find true love on a planet far from Earth?

Tamed by an Alien Warlord is Book 2 in the Fated Mates of the Ferlaern Warriors Series. This standalone, full-length romance has on-the-page heat, aliens who look and act alien, a guaranteed happily ever after, no cheating, and no cliffhanger. Look for the series on Amazon.

Chapter 1
RAYNE

As setting sunlight bled across the sky in streaks of blood red and gold, I moved quickly across the forest floor, keeping my footsteps light. Though they hadn't made it clear why, I'd been told more than once by the Ferlaern warriors not to leave the canopy village without an escort. If I was caught, I could get into trouble.

But an escort? As if one of the guards had time to follow me while I examined trees.

I snorted, and a pesky fly buzzing around my head took off as if *I* was the threat.

The Ferlaern had to be overreacting.

Besides, I wouldn't be down here long. I'd get my soil samples and return to the village before it was time for me to pick up my five-year-old daughter, Missy, from her play date with a friend.

This couldn't wait.

The mighty aresk trees were dying, and I was determined to find out why. Even now, I could see a sickly yellow cast to their leaves. The smaller branches that snapped at a subtle twist of my fingers instead of bending. Was this part of the tree's lifecycle? I didn't know, but I was determined to find out.

I wasn't an arborist; back on Earth, I worked for a landscaping company. But I had an affinity for trees. They knew it, and they thrived under my touch.

A thumping sound behind me sent me spinning. My heart leaped up into my throat, and I peered around, taking in the dense vegetation encroaching on the narrow path.

When a small creature that vaguely looked like a tiny cat scooted from one side of the path to the other, my pulse slowed.

"It's nothing," I whispered. "Just an alien kitty." I turned and continued down the trail. "A cute alien kitty but not a true threat."

I hoped.

Partway through this section of the forest, I stopped beside one of the taller trees towering over me at least two-hundred-feet. If I stretched my arms out and hugged it, I'd barely span one side.

Our Clan lived in the canopy of these trees. They sheltered our homes and protected us from the weather.

Us. I used the term loosely. I was an Earthling who arrived on this planet a few weeks ago to settle. The new wild west, my friend Piper called it. Our settlement in a deep valley several days flight from here hadn't lasted long after the duskhorde attacked. The damn, creepy aliens had a taste for flesh and were determined to capture Earth women for breeding or supper. We escaped their attack with the help of the Ferlaern warriors who'd arrived to help us build. After most of our possessions burned, the Ferlaern brought us to where they spent their winters high in the mountains where they set us up in vacant homes. Domits, they were called, big, hollow, pear-shaped blossoms dangling from the trees. Each contained a living area and two bedrooms. No kitchen, but who wanted to cook? We all ate in a central domit. I still wasn't sure who did the cooking but I probably needed to find out as I should take my turn with kitchen duty.

Later.

The wildest part of our living situation was the trundiers, the winged creatures Piper insisted looked like hornets (she was right). Ferlaern warriors rode them like dragons, though I'd yet to see any shoot flames. The ginormous beasts nested in the canopy as well, and right now, their young were hatching.

I ran my fingers along the tree's bark, feeling for loose areas, then stooped down to examine the soil mulched around the roots. So far, I didn't see anything unusual, but I'd just started my investigation.

Holding the short sword I'd kinda, sorta borrowed from my favorite Ferlaern warrior who might not be too happy if he found out, I left the first tree and crept closer to the specific one I needed to examine. Around me, ferns at least twice my height slow-danced in the breeze, and a plumed endla bird hopped up onto a waist-high rock and squawked at me, pissed off I walked through its territory. As if its fangs weren't enough to make me keep my distance, it expanded its tail feathers like a nightmarish peacock. Each of the feathers was tipped with a narrow blade. At least they couldn't throw them—as far as I knew.

I scooted around the angry bird but froze when I heard a subtle rustle in the woods behind me.

My lungs cut off as I looked around, but I didn't see anything but the bird hopping off the rock and scooting into the underbrush. With a frown, I huffed out a breath and continued toward the tree. As I got closer, I studied the bark and the roots partly covered with ages of dead vegetation.

"Poor baby," I said, stroking the tree.

It made a purring sound. Like really, a solid purr, which was kinda cute.

"Are you talking to me?" I whispered, gliding my fingers along the tree again. "You like this, don't you?" I'd never had a tree respond to my touch before, but this was a new world with new creatures and plants. If the trees enjoyed a good pat, I was all in.

Something skittered over my sneaker, and I leaped backward, my arms flailing. My heart erupted up into my throat and for a second, I thought it I'd cough it up.

The tiny cat-like creature I saw earlier on the path stood on a nearby root jutting from the soil, staring up at me. Only a little bigger than my palm, it had four legs with puffy fur, a floofy tail, and two very tall, pointy ears with tufts on the top. Its long snout wiggled like a mole's and it skittered forward and dug its claws into the canvas of my sneakers, thankfully not slicing through.

"Who are you?" I asked it in the voice I reserved to lull babies.

It purred and tried to climb my pants.

"Oh, so you're the one who was making that sound, not the tree."

It tipped its head back and studied me before it essentially grinned, revealing long, thin fangs. A lot of things had fangs or tusks here on Ferlaern, and tusks were growing on me. Especially Durran's tusks. I kept imagine him behind me, his arms wrapped around my waist while he nipped at my shoulder with them. An impossible dream since he fled in the opposite direction whenever I came near.

Lifting the alien kitten, I held it aloft on my palm.

"What's your name, little kitty?" I asked.

Its nose wiggled, and it sniffed my palm before licking it. That tickled, and I chuckled.

Leaves rustled behind me again. Pulling the kitten close to my neck, I peered over my shoulder with fear raking down my spine.

There were many unknown creatures on Ferlaern, and I wasn't eager to meet any of them outside the kitten, but nothing moved behind me.

This reminded me I needed to get my mission over with and get back up into the canopy.

With the kitten in one hand, my bag hitched over my shoulder, and my sword held aloft, I moved around the tree, examining the bark and roots elbowing up through the moist, mulched soil.

The kitty purred and cocked its head, peering past me, into the forest. Its tiny blue eyes widened and it leaped off my hand and plopped on the ground then scurried around the side of the tree.

"Come back," I said, hurrying after it.

A tap on my spine made me shriek. I spun and thrust my sword forward.

Durran deflected it to the side with an easy swipe.

While a few of the women watched this Ferlaern warrior with frowns, I stared at him like he was a chocolate sundae with whipped cream and a cherry on top. I wanted to glide my fingertips along the history written in the scars on his face, though I doubted he'd ever let me.

He scowled. "That's my sword." He took it from my limp hand and twisted it one way then the other, examining it like he thought I hacked brush with it to purposefully dull the blade. "Where did you get it?"

"I…borrowed it." Crap, crap, crap. I was going to get into trouble now.

"Borrow implies permission." He bit out the words.

My lips thinned. "So, I extra borrowed it."

His scowl deepened, creating larger grooves in his face as the segments gave way to his scars. Made up of burnished gold, his skin gleamed dully in the sunlight. His black-as-night hair was shot through with deep purple strands, and I ached to run my fingers through it. Something else I doubt he'd allow. "There is no such thing as extra borrowing," he said.

Yeah, well, I invented the term.

"I'm sorry," I said, aiming for contrite. "I couldn't come down here without protection, and you sorta left your sword lying around."

"Where?" His thick brow knitted together.

"I, um, well, when you left it with Berrand for repairs, I adopted it."

"Swords are not tiny creatures to be adopted."

Like the kitty? I needed to find the poor thing and take it home. Missy would love it. Hell, I loved it already. Unless Durran was offering, I needed someone to snuggle up to in bed each night.

"Would you have let me borrow it if I asked?" I was truly curious about his answer. "I bet you would stomped away without giving me an answer."

He blinked as if he didn't know how to take me. Welcome to my life, buddy. I sure didn't know how to take him.

"You can have your sword back. I'm all done with it," I said, my throat tightening as it always did when I was close to him. Like someone hit a switch, I became a mix of teenage giddy and straight-up, womanly lust. "What, err, are you doing here?" I carefully tucked my bag of tools and sampling equipment behind my thighs. Because his heady scent surrounded me, making me eager to press myself against him, I leaned against the enormous tree. Actually, I supported myself against the tree. What was it about this guy? He could turn my knees to mush with one glance. I was a twenty-eight-year-old woman with a young daughter, for heaven's sake. Not a blushing virgin.

"Hunting," he answered shortly.

"No luck, huh?" My face colored the second I spoke. Way to make him feel bad about returning to the village empty-handed.

"No."

Ah, now this was the Durran I knew and, well, liked. He was big on sex appeal, small on conversation. The one time we were alone together for more than two seconds, he said nothing, just stared at me.

"Do you hunt often?" I asked to make conversation.

"Sometimes."

Hey, we were making progress, moving from simple stares to limited sentences. Within a hundred years, we might work up to complete paragraphs.

"I see," I said.

He studied my face so I took a second to check him out, too. From the first time I met him, I was drawn to this alien, but so far, he seemed oblivious to my dubious charms. And let me tell you, I turned them on, trying to draw his attention. Short of dancing in front of him naked, I'd used the usual methods, including sidling up to him and talking about the weather. Offering to fix him a plate of food in the community dining domit. Asking him to repair my unbroken domit door—while he mumbled something I took as agreement, he'd yet to stop by to "fix" it.

He slunk away each time I spoke.

"What are you hunting?" I asked, tipping my head back to look up at him. At seven-one or two, I was eyeball level to his nicely muscled chest. The tips of his six-inch horns jutted upward through his black and purple hair, and I wanted to grab onto his horns and run my fingertips down their thick lengths. His locks hung to the middle of his back and some women might be turned off by a guy with hair longer than hers. Uh-uh. All I could picture was the strands gliding across my naked skin while he strained above me.

My skin flamed. I needed to drag my brain out of the gutter. The chance of sex between me and Durran was as possible as me becoming President of this planet and let me tell you, no one was suggesting I run for election.

"Liscards," he said abruptly. "I was about to hunt liscards."

"For dinner?"

"No one eats liscards."

"Then why hunt them?"

"We need to keep the population down so they don't eat the trundier hatchlings." His feet shifted, and I could almost picture him telling himself he was done with this conversation and me, pivoting, and running all get out in the opposite direction.

"You're the one in charge of the trundiers, right?" I asked, hoping if I focused on his job, he'd remain grounded in my vicinity.

A swallow worked its way down his throat, and his deep green eyes strayed everywhere but toward me. "I'm head trainer." His thick, husky voice sent electric tingles down my spine. The effect he had on me really wasn't fair.

Leaves crunched behind him and something released a low, growling sound like two boulders grinding together.

I cocked my head, wondering what it might be.

Durran spun, his hand seamlessly pulling a short sword from the scabbard on his chest.

The ferns swayed and branches broke as something came near.

"Hide, Rayne," he hissed.

A giant crocodile burst from the bushes and stomped toward us with its fangs dripping goo and its claws churning the soil.

You can get your copy of Tamed by an Alien Warlord on Amazon.